Paw Prints
Through The Years

Jean C. Keating

Art by

Beverly S. Abbott

Astra Publishers

Williamsburg, Virginia

Text copyrighted by Jean C. Keating
Art copyrighted by Beverly S. Abbott

Library of Congress Catalog Card Number: 2003114016
ISBN # 0-9674016-3-1

Printing 2004
10 9 8 7 6 5 4 3 2 1

Front Cover: *Butterflies In Motion* by Bev Abbott
Back Cover: *A Tail of Two Pots* by Bev Abbott
Astra logo by Beverly S. Abbott, For Arts Sake

Web design and hosting by Virginia Networks: rdennis@richmond.net

Copies available from the publisher:

Astra Publications
209 Matoaka Court
Williamsburg, VA 23185
(757) 220-3385
www.astrapublishers.com

Acknowledgements

This didn't begin as a novel, so my patient friend and wonderful editor, Mary Ann Burns, has been forced by necessity to read and reread several versions of the same text. Her dedication and careful editing have smoothed this story into the flowing saga that it is. I am deeply grateful for her help and friendship.

Dot Bryant persevered with the formatting despite a terrible hurricane named Isabel who challenged us all. Formatting and editing files with only a generator to power the computer and lights were a labor of love and much appreciated by this writer.

I am indebted to my wonderful critique group members who listened, commented, recommended improvements, and supported my efforts with many kind words and encouraging compliments. Rick and Emeline Bailey, Bob Black, Richard Corwin, Hugh Davis, Joe Guion, Virginia Ladd, Ed Matson and Kitty Moore: thanks for listening and improving this story.

I don't think this introduction would be complete without sharing the tale behind a single page of this book. By candlelight and generator, a near final version was produced that had some thorns, not the least of which were two page #84's. I undertook to fuss and fumble the renumbering of the pages since Dot Bryant was on the West Coast in a meeting. In the process I got rid of not one but both page #84's. My dear friend and artist Bev Abbott stepped in to produce a graphic of two of my dogs to put on the page, and her husband Ira dealt with the digital imaging and transmission, as he had with the color plates and endpages. The final insult was when my internet carrier followed the newly supplied page #84 with a note that my mailbox was too full and I wouldn't be allowed to receive any more mail if I didn't clean out my box. I began to think that page was jinxed!

Last, but certainly not least, I extend my gratitude and love to the past and present members of the Astra pack for their inspirations that made this book possible.

Books from Astra Publishers

Amorous Accident: A Dog's Eye View of Murder by Jean C. Keating

Pawprints On My Heart: Edited by Jean C. Keating, Illustrated by Beverly S. Abbott

Mercy Me by John Atkinson

DEDICATED TO

Mark Sullivan, D.V. M.

*..... doctor, protector and friend of the
Astra gang*

Illustrations

Endsheets: Am/Can/Mex/Hon/Int'l/Lat Am Ch/BIS Int's/G.C.M./C.G.C. Champion Debonair Scooter Deluxe [*Scooter Carmichael*], PCA SOM and Champion Astra's Onyx Original [*Nikki Keating*]

Frontispiece: Astra's Ivory Illusion [*Ivory Keating*]

Center color plates:

#1 Champion Debonair Calvin Kline [*Vinnie Gell*], PCA SOD

#2 Champion Astra's Fallon of Bow Creek [*Fallon Keating*]

#3 top: Champion Debonair Maaca Choice [*Maaca Keating*]
    bottom: Astra's Mischief Maaca [*Mischief Keating*, as a puppy and as an adult]

#4 Astra's Winter Waltz [*Windi Keating*]

#5 top: Walden's Garsun Beag [*Teddy Grey*]
    bottom: Walden's Three Wood [*Nigel Rosenberg*]

#6 top: Astra's Divine Diva [*DeeDee Keating*]
        Champion Astra's Designated Driver [*Driver Keating*]
    Bottom: Astra's Velvet Victory [*Toto Demhearter*]

#7 Champion Astra's Designated Driver [*Driver Keating*]

#8 Astra's Happy Habit [*Happy Keating*]

Page 84: Astra's Hardly Holy [*Holy Keating*] and
        Champion Astra's Brainy Bear [*Bear Keating*]

Paw Prints
Through The Years

Happiness Is A
Dog Named Vinnie

I don't know about other women's intuition, but mine was nonexistent on that long-ago morning. I had no hint, no tingle of a notion that the events of that day would bring such a change in my life.

It certainly needed changing. The emotional severance of divorce was bad enough. The daunting task of splitting property and possessions acquired over 19 years of marriage had exceeded my abilities to cope. I was deep in my own private pity party, convinced that I was the only one who'd ever been hurt by such a tragedy. I finally consented to go with my friend to a dog show in Virginia Beach only because she just wouldn't take no for an answer.

Even while I vowed I would never depend on another human being for the rest of my life and never enter into the joint ownership of anything, some appreciation for the importance of a friend remained. So I dragged myself to the show, but stubbornly promised myself I wouldn't enjoy it.

Fate, with perhaps a helping hand from my guardian angel, decreed otherwise. 'Across a crowded room'—in this

1

case the floor of the indoor dog show in Norfolk—I spotted HIM. Soft, expressive brown eyes that held a mixture of intelligence, compassion and bubbling mischief locked with mine. HE didn't seem to mind that I was frowning and stumbling along. He cocked his head and nodded in my direction, seeming to invite me to come closer. Captivated, I stepped on one woman's toes and fell over a gentle mastiff headed for another ring.

Long black-and-brown fringes softened large ears that rotated like radar dishes at the sound of my greeting. A wide white nose band and blaze added dazzling brilliance to his flashing eyes as he lifted first one dainty front foot and then another from the lap of the man who held him, dancing his happiness at life. A long white plume of a tail fanned his human's face and moved the entire rear end of his body with its energetic greeting. I had seen a lot of dogs wag their tails. That was a first for seeing one wag his ears also. And what large beautiful ears they were! I forgot I was mad at the world. All I could see, feel, think about at that moment was the deliriously happy and beautifully expressive bundle of silken fur that charged the space around him with positive energy.

Such was my first meeting with a papillon. In French, the name means butterfly. That morning the large erect ears and trailing fringes of this little charmer fanned the air with all the grace, beauty and lightness of the delicate and colorful insects for which the breed was named.

I managed to learn his name was Vinnie before his amused human excused himself to take the little bundle of happiness into the ring. I grabbed the vacated chair at ringside to watch my newest interest show off.

The indoor dog show was noisy. It wasn't the twelve hundred or so dogs that created the din, it was the more than twelve hundred people there. Vinnie didn't seem to mind the noise in spite of his keen hearing. When his human put him on the floor, he circled and danced on dainty feet, following his human into the exhibition ring. His little white paws seemed to glide effortlessly across the black mat which formed a border and a diagonal pattern on the ring floor. When not moving he would stand with feet planted, tail constantly in motion, and head, ears, and eyes *talking* with his human or the judge. His entire body proclaimed his joy at doing what he was doing and in being alive.

Even in the protected environment of a dog show ring, accidents can happen. And one did that day. As the group of dogs and handlers paraded around the ring, the human behind Vinnie stumbled on the mat. She fell forward and nearly stepped on him. With cat-quick reflexes and strong patellas, the little athlete leaped up and away from the danger. My most enduring and delightful memory of this beautiful dog was that of an airborne aerialist. All four feet and body were in the air, hair fluffed out by the wind currents around him as his trajectory carried him up, over and down again to the mat. He quickly recovered himself and continued the smooth forward gait of his performance.

I was too ignorant of show procedures at that time to know whether he won or not. I know that I would have given him all the ribbons.

By the time Vinnie and his human finished their performance and returned to their ringside chair, I had already decided that I wanted a papillon. I managed to overcome my fascination with that little bundle of energy long enough to obtain a business card that told me how to contact Vinnie's breeders and to learn that his other, longer name was Debonair Calvin Klein.

I didn't give his owner/handler/breeder long enough to return home before I was talking to his wife on the phone about a papillon for my very own.

I left the show in a far different frame of mind. One tiny bundle of flashing white and mahogany showed me the way.

Jean C. Keating

It was time to let go of an old life and 'reach for the stars.' Suddenly the chore of property settlements was just a job to be assessed and completed. My focus was on a new life and love.

In time Vinnie's half sister, my beloved Maaca, would come to share my life and be my first show dog and champion. Vinnie's daughter Fallon would follow a few years later. Together these two relations of Vinnie would be the foundation of a clan which over the years would come to be known as the butterflies of Astra [Latin for star]. For more than twenty years these two and their descendants have brought warmth, love, laughter and happiness into every moment of my life.

There is a wise axiom that 'happiness is a choice'. Vinnie obviously chose to enjoy life, the scene around him that day, and to warmly draw all about him into his web of excitement.

I think dogs were sent by God to teach us to make the most of each day. I'm glad I took the hint.

4

Beginning Again

I hung up the phone from talking with Vinnie's breeder and danced around the room. My two housemates looked at me in shock from their chosen places on the sofa. Miss Pittypat wagged her tail slowly before returning to her usual chore of the afternoon, the three-hour nap she required to furnish her with the energy for our before-dinner walk. A blond, plump and sweet chihuahua and pekinese mix, she had no premonition of the change to her life that phone call would produce. Sir Sable sailed off the sofa to jump around me and bark at my excited behavior, then tore into the den to retrieve his favorite toy. The stuffed bear was too big for his little chihuahua mouth to carry, but he managed to drag it back and push it toward me with his front legs on the rug, rump in air, inviting me to play. While I grabbed the bear, shook it in front of his face, and tossed it a short distance away for him to retrieve, I told him that he would soon have a young papillon as a playmate and I hoped he was prepared to share his toys. He made no promises. But as fate would have it, one other little buddy would join our family group before the gleefully anticipated papillon.

5

Jean C. Keating

An elderly chihuahua-manchester terrier mix had been dumped at the local shelter several weeks before. She was sweet and trusting despite being neglected and possibly actively abused. Her nails were so long they curved under and her short, black coat resembled a scrub pad more than hair. Any gait faster than a slow stroll was usually accomplished on three legs, for her left patella was so bad she held it up and hopped rather than trying to use the leg. Small dogs generally have a better chance of finding a second-chance home, but this little mix, who had been named Peanut by the shelter, had been passed over for younger, healthier candidates. Despite being featured in a newspaper ad and taken to a local retirement home for exposure, little Peanut had not captured the interest of a new owner. A friend at the shelter called to say time had run out for this trusting oldie and she would be put down unless someone offered her a home immediately.

I reasoned that since Sir Sable would soon have a young, playful papillon for a companion, Miss Pittypat would need someone to sleep away the hours with her, so the blond bomber and I went to the shelter to collect Peanut.

Can anything prepare one for the look in the eyes of an old dog that has tried too hard to please, been rejected so much, expected little, and been given only the scraps of life? Sable and Pittypat had come to me as exuberant and out-going puppies, had been pampered and coddled during their entire lives. The first days with Peanut were a far different challenge. She didn't want to displease anyone for fear of being rejected again. Sable the scamp took rapid advantage of the situation and stole her food every chance he had. Peanut would just back away from her dish and let him have her food. A bath terrified her, as did her first vet visit. Even the bed seemed to frighten her. It didn't help that Pittypat contested every pillow and had to be convinced to share. It would take two years before Peanut was truly comfortable sleeping in the big, king-size bed with Sable, Pittypat, me and the young pap who would come to join our pack.

Peanut was insistent about only one thing, her participation in outings. Despite autumn's chill and a bum leg, she was adamant about joining our merry band for evening walks. A few dog sweaters provided the warmth that her poor coat didn't, but I often ended up carrying her most of the way back. Hopping on three legs was exhausting enough. Sable made it worse by circling her during the walks and bumping into her.

Sometime during the fall, a new family moved into the next block with a huge black dog. At least I think it was huge. Its head certainly was. It appeared that the owner or owners lived on the second floor of a two story house near the College of William and Mary and lacked yard space. Whatever the situation, the dog seemed to be confined to a front room on the second floor. Or rather most of his body was. He'd managed to tear a hole in the screen and push his huge block of a black head outside the screen to bark ferociously at our little walking group as we past. I took to carrying a spray bottle filled with bitter apple solution just in case the body should follow the head through the window and out to the street where we walked. Pittypat laid back her ears each time we passed near the house. Sable tucked his tail between his legs and dragged back on the leash whether the barking head appeared or not. Peanut just refused to walk past the house and had to be picked up and carried.

As autumn slipped into winter, our fearsome four presented a silly caricature of an inept juggling act during our walks. I staggered along trying to hold on to the leashes of two dogs, while carrying a third in one hand and a spray-bottle at the ready in the other.

Jean C. Keating

Christmas was fast approaching with no further word of our hoped-for papillon, but the four of us managed to enjoy our holidays just the same. I bought a small tree and decided to decorate for the holidays for the first time since my divorce. Pittypat and Peanut supervised the trimming of the small tree between skirmishes over squatters' rights to the ornament box's lid. Sable actively helped by claiming every other ornament as his private toy. I could have trimmed the tree faster with a room full of octopuses.

Since the dogs had come to be such a large part of my life, to be in fact my immediate family, I decided that Christmas cards would be written in the voice of one of them, and so assigned Pittypat, the senior canine, the task of 'writing' the cards. If family and friends were surprised to receive communications from a dog, they were too pleased to hear anything at all from me to complain about the means. And so another year passed into memory and brought a shining, new one with challenges to meet, problems to solve, and adventures to enjoy together.

December, 1981

Dear Friends and Family,

Mama Jean has assigned me the job of writing the Christmas cards this year. This may be a ploy to keep me from fighting with my new sister Peanut

over the lid to the Christmas ornaments. It gives me the chance to get in my own ideas, so I couldn't say no.

Mama Jean went off to a dog show earlier in the year and came back all excited about getting a new member of the family. But I don't think Peanut was what she planned. At any rate, Peanut is an awful pain. She has no manners and eats just about anything. So we don't have food around all the time because piggy Peanut just eats until she's sick. We just get fed twice a day. Period! Sable says she can't play with any of his toys, but she doesn't care. Just wants to sleep on my pillows!

Oh, Mama says I should just wish you a Merry Christmas and a Happy New Year from all of us. Including Peanut? Do I gotta? Oh, shucks!

Pittypat

9

The Arrival of the Queen

The bleakness of January was brightened by several funny letters in response to the Christmas card from a dog. One cousin wrote to say she didn't know whether to send the name of a good psychologist or just take comfort in the fact that I was at least communicating again. The long awaited letter regarding my papillon puppy arrived with the new year also, and sent me digging for new knowledge. The letter brought an offer for my adoption of a beautiful black-and-white beauty named Maaca, along with her pedigree and pictures of her standing by the pool.

Now I think of myself as reasonably intelligent. Or I did until faced with a six-generation pedigree. Oh, boy! I worked through the easier parts. I'd already learned that long names generally comprised a kennel prefix that indicated who bred the dog and a unique name that signified the dog. I was helped in identifying the conformation champions by the fact that these appeared in red and in caps on the pedigree, so the 'CH' in front of names was understandable. I despaired at ever getting the strings of letters at the end of each dog's name straight. Entries like 'CD' and 'CDX' became clearer after

10

reading up on obedience competitions. Strings of information like 'DOM' and 'SOD' after names left me feeling frustrated and foolish. In the coming years, I would learn that these last two signified Dam of Merit and Sire of Distinction respectively, titles awarded by the Papillon Club of America to signify milestones in champion get produced by these beautiful dogs. But in the beginning, I just knew that my friend Vinnie's father was a 'SOD' so it must mean something great.

Finally, when it came to trying to understand why some half-brothers and half-sisters were bred to each other, and why the same names appeared in more than one generation, I gave up the book research and called a good friend who bred and showed dachshunds.

Knowledge and experience are wonderful things. My friend took about two minutes to view the pedigree and answered all my queries with a single brief suggestion. "Go get the little girl, and count yourself very lucky."

So I did. I settled most of the arrangements by mail, and, on Valentine's Day, drove to Maryland to get my darling Maaca. Her full name was Debonair Maaca [pronounced 'Make A'] Choice.

Like Vinnie, she was sired by American and Canadian Champion Kinrennie Udell. The 'SOD'. Her dam was another beautiful champion named Heidi [CH D'Ronde's High Hope]. While I learned in a few months that the 'DOD' after Heidi's name signified she had whelped more than ten champions, it would be many years before I would really begin to comprehend what an astounding feat it was for a pap bitch to produce that many champions because of the small litter size usual in this breed. At this time, I only knew that this little one was rare and precious and I felt very honored to have been offered the chance to share her life.

Unlike Vinnie, she was not all happy kisses and welcoming tail-wags. Friendship was one thing; her half-brother Vinnie could be casual about that. Entrusting her life to a stranger was another thing altogether, and this dainty, black-and-white beauty seemed to know it. The deep brown eyes she trained on me were intelligent but wary. At ten and a half months, she was no fat, cuddly baby but an elegant young lady who already knew her worth in the world. She posed regally just out of reach of my hand and eyed me critically during the entire time I was consulting with her breeders and signing the final papers of her adoption. She did consent to being the subject of a demonstration of correct brushing techniques and feet trimming conducted for my enlightenment. But her queenly attitude left no doubt that I was being evaluated by her royal regalness.

Freshly brushed and trimmed, she danced away with elegant neck arched and big ears flashing their independence. Little white feet seemed to glide over the floor as she returned to play with her kennel mates, including my first-love Vinnie.

We were invited to spend the night at her breeders and Maaca went upstairs with me into the guest room. She eyed the bed with a calculating gleam in her eyes, finally walked over to lick my hand in acceptance before demurely trying out the new crate and bedding I'd brought along. I guess it was satisfactory, because she slept through the night without any fussing and made the four-hour trip back home the next day sleeping soundly.

We went for a brief walk before I took Maaca into her new home to meet the rest of the crew. Peanut barked ferociously at her, seeking to defend the house against an unknown invader with the dedication only a rescue dog seems to feel. Maaca ignored her, gently shouldered her aside and walked straight into a nose-to-nose face-off with Pittypat. Sable bounced around to the rear, tried a butt sniff and got chastised sharply by the queen. After a few grumbles, Pittypat backed off and Maaca started a leisurely exploration of her new digs.

Feeding schedules had to be adjusted to reflect

Paw Prints Through The Years

Maaca's expectations of her accustomed dinner of liver and ground beef with rice, human variety if you please. This idea was readily supported by Pittypat, Sable and Peanut and in exchange, Maaca never complained that dry kibble wasn't available all the time, since free feeding had proved impossible with Peanut around.

I worried about the impact of a fourth dog on evening outings. Four leashes plus a spray bottle were getting to be a little more than I felt capable of handling. I need not have fretted. The first night we approached the house with the loudly barking dog's head in the second floor window, Maaca responded with a piercing scream that rivaled the fire station alarm bell rather than even remotely resembling any bark I'd ever heard. The offending head was withdrawn so quickly that part of the torn screen was pulled into the upstairs room behind the disappearing black skull.

Unfortunately, Maaca's scream did about as much damage to Peanut's nerves as the barking dog in the upper window had achieved, so I still had to carry our little cripple home in my arms. I was laughing all the way at the response of this regal lady to the black dog's challenge to her walk.

We enrolled in training classes offered by our local all-breed dog club. Maaca was the star of the class, but it soon became apparent that I had no talent or interest in actually entering a ring and showing a dog. The additional sixty-mile commute to classes on top of a hundred mile commute to work each day was a small part of the problem. It left too little time for anything else, including the three other trusting companions in my life. Moreover, I wanted to watch and analyze what was going on with this delightful little personality, but not make a fool of myself by actually going into the ring with her. We tried a few shows, which she won, no thanks to me. She walked a straight line; I mostly fell over my own feet. A quick call to Maaca's breeders brought instant help and the name of a lovely handler to guide this

13

Jean C. Keating

beautiful girl in her show career. Two circuits and five weeks
later, this showy little imp earned the right to put a 'CH'
signifying champion before her name. She was eleven and a
half months old.

With Maaca in the ring with an accomplished handler, I
was free to sit at ringside and delight in the intelligence and
innate showmanship of this little dog. She was handed to
the handler at ringside, so there was little time for training by
her handler. Yet she knew just whom to play up to. Her
eager, expressive eyes and constantly moving ears and tail
were always focused on the judge.

At home, the interaction of the four very different
canine personalities intrigued and delighted me. Pittypat
was older, established as the senior dog, but calm and
unassuming. She wouldn't give up her pillow or favorite toy
to any of the other canines. But she never offered to fight
about it. She was too laid back to really want to push about
anything. She'd just sit or hold wherever she was or
whatever she had.

Peanut never tried to take anything, always responded
with a submissive posture if conflict over space or food
occurred. Sable, the only male and the one closest to
Maaca's age, was always pushing, always trying to get
whatever anyone of the girls might have just for the pure joy
of initiating a reaction, but it was a lot of noise and little
more. Maaca quietly or cunningly got what she wanted.

If Pittypat had the favorite spot on the sofa, Maaca
would wander into another room and a few minutes later
bark at nothing. Peanut, ever ready to defend her much
appreciated home, would rush to Maaca to support her alert.
Sable would then join the party with his furious barking since
he seemed to love the sound of his own yip yaps. As soon
as Pittypat joined the group in response to the false alert,
Maaca would make a swift end run back to the sofa and
grab the favorite spot just vacated by Pittypat.

14

Paw Prints Through The Years

It was a source of endless fascination to me to see the cognitive reasoning exhibited by this first of many papillon companions, although the noise from such group barking sessions did little to enhance my TV viewing or my phone conversations.

Language of The Eyes

Mankind, in his arrogance, belittles other species as lacking the gift of a spoken language. Considering how many words some people can use to convey little or no information, or to lie and deceive, I sometimes wonder what reason humans have to brag. Dogs talk with their whole body, with ears and tail, with posturing, and especially with their eyes. Moreover, they never lie.

Any dog which has ever been handed table scraps from his master's plate learns quickly the art of begging with soft, liquid brimming eyes for more, and more, and still more. When dogs turn eyes filled with compassion on another of their pack, the intensity of their tenderness humbles my efforts in comparison.

Peanut was terrified of storms. Superior hearing was a curse for her, for she always sensed thunderstorms coming before they left Richmond, which is fifty miles west of our home. Some evenings I would read in bed before turning out the light, attended by four small bodies scattered over the other two-thirds of the bed. My first notice of an approaching storm would be a whimper from Peanut which would grow in

16

volume and pitch until she would be huddled against me, digging into the sheet in an attempt to get under my body. Her three canine friends would rouse from their own sleep to crowd around her, their eyes mirroring her pain and brimming with sympathy. Neither my wrapping her in a blanket and holding her nor their surrounding her with their bodies did much to lessen her fear, but it was not for want of their trying to convey their love and caring to her.

Pittypat's expressions seemed to always be trusting, filled with happy anticipations of a meal, a pat on the head, a scratch behind the ear, or with heightened glee at hearing the word, 'walk' or 'out'. Sable's eyes were almost always filled with merriment, since he was generally plotting ways in which to entice the three girls to play or to aggravate them when they declined his overtures. Despite my assumptions that Maaca would serve as his playmate, she proved to be very reserved and mature for her chronological age. She mostly declined to enter into his free-for-all, toy-tugging games. Peanut's eyes seemed always to be filled with gratitude that she'd come to a warm and caring place, one with plenty of food and fresh water. Except for the fearful pleading that showed in times of thunderstorms and nail clippings, her countenance was soft and contented. She was a happy follower so long as the B word [BATH] didn't enter into the conversation.

Maaca was another entity entirely. She had so many expressions and eye signals, she kept me busy trying to read them all. She frequently displayed an unmistakable look of frustration and disgust when confronted with certain breeds of dogs. She seemed to regard the snuffling sound, which is a part of the normal breathing of breeds with pushed in noses, as a challenge. Bulldogs came in for a lot of suspicious looks. She would wheel and misbehave in any ring which contained them nearby. The Toy group ring was a challenge. She eyed many of the breeds in the group with distrust, and even managed to growl at a pug that came too near during one show. Fortunately, the judge didn't hear her. Both her handler and I learned to watch her expressions carefully. Unfortunately the English language dictates that papillon comes just before pekingese in lineups for the group, so it was impossible to avoid having a snuffling peke behind her in a lot of group showings if the judge dictated that the breeds line up in alphabetic order. I always hoped the innocent, little bundles of peke fur that followed her about the Toy Group ring at many shows never saw the petulant glances that she threw their way.

Airedales she would not abide. An airedale lunged at her at her fourth dog show. It wasn't even the dog's fault. His handler was trying to show off to the judge in the Airedale ring that his specimen possessed the proper terrier-like qualities by siccing him at Maaca. Big mistake! It was the WRONG toy dog to pick for that trick! She gave him her fire-alarm scream that had terrified the black head in the upstairs window on our walks. Said Airedale quailed behind handler and almost dumped the fool on his rump. Show people, including the veterinarian on call, came running to help the 'mortally injured dog' only to find me holding a very much alive and angered Miss Maaca-the Lion-Hearted. Eyes blazing her defiance and small-but-determined body struggling to get out of my arms, she was obstinately focused on getting across the floor to the other dog. She was almost eleven months old at the time, but she never forgot, forgave, or ceased trying to tell any Airedale she met of her private feud with them. Unlike her mistress, she never confused them with Lakeland Terriers.

During the fall show season, my concerns began to focus more urgently on a possible mate for Maaca. I'd been poring over books on breeding and discussing the issues with Maaca's breeder. All sources seemed to agree that the best time for a first breeding would be the third season. She would reach her third season sometime in late October or early November, so my ringside observations began to include critical evaluations of male entries for possible husbands. The few that I singled out for consideration were treated with disdain by the queen.

Her eyes were always afire with delight when a judge approached with a ribbon, however. She loved ribbons! We attended a few matches of my local club as exhibition champions because they gave lovely trophy rosettes. At one exhibition she treated the ringmaster to a look that could only be described as the 'look that could kill.' Unlike judges, exhibition ringmasters generally read from a brief bio about the dog being gaited around the ring, describing accomplishments of the dog to the crowd in the name of educating those attending about purebred dogs. The poor man was busy sharing with the crowd of spectators some very flattering ad lib comments to flush out Maaca's brief bio, explaining that puppy champions were rare and signified especially correct and beautiful dogs. Well, Madam Queenie didn't understand his talk, however complimentary to her. What she understood was that she had done her prance around the ring, done her pose on the table, batted her eyes and flashed her tail at him, and he'd not given her the RIBBON. For this exhibition program, I was at the other end of her leash in the ring with her and trying not to explode in laughter at her furious glares at the ringmaster.

Some weeks later we were back at a regular show and I was again sitting at ringside watching Maaca's performance while sizing up the males at the show as possible husbands. I had tried to be very analytical about strengths and weaknesses in this delightful little minx that had brought so much entertainment and pleasure into my life. Her front structure was straight, strong and true and I wasn't interested in any suitor that didn't match her in strength there. Top line was level and true, tail and ear set correct.

Jean C. Keating

Likewise her rear movement and reach of stride was smooth and fluid. Her white blaze was pencil thin however. And there is no such thing to a papillon owner as too much fringe. So I wanted a mate that would possess all of her positive qualities but have a wide blaze and lots of ear fringe. I was disappointed to find nothing I liked as husband material at the show.

I passed over a six-plus year old and graying, sable-and-white champion. His ear fringe and coat were showing the signs of aging, and though he moved with grace and beauty still, I was focused on fringe, fringe, and more fringe! Not little miss know-it-all. She began to flirt with this oldie more than she did the judge. Knowing her usual habits with regard to judges, I decided that such unusual behavior needed further investigation.

The show catalog gave me the oldie's name, the name of sire, dam and owner. I initiated a conversation with the handler after the breed showing finished, but did not commit myself. I was mildly amused that Maaca seemed to be enamored with an 'older man', but at least conceded that she had the good taste to pick one who was a champion and whose sire and dam were champions also. Moreover, her 'older man's' sire was also a Canadian champion. At this point, I comprehended very little of the impressive credentials of Maaca's choice. CH Jeja's Huger, owned by Jessie Johnson of South Carolina, was sired by American and Canadian CH Jaclair's Doodles of Josandre, CDX out of CH. Jeja's Mam'zelle.

Back home with my nose buried in reference material from the Papillon Club of America, I could only chuckle with amusement and marvel at the wisdom of her choice. Huger was already a Papillon Club of America Sire of Merit, having sired five champions. His dam Mam'zelle was the mother of champions already with Huger and another to her credit, and in the years to come would whelp a total of four champions to become a PCA Dame of Merit. As for Huger's sire, well, one could write an entire book about him. He was a PCA Sire of Distinction, with twenty published champions, exceeded only by the sixty-odd of his own grandsire, Gowdy. Doodles held not only dual conformation championships, but American and Canadian obedience championships as well. He won four Best in Shows during an age when papillons were little recognized. He was the only obedience titled papillon to win Best in Show, the youngest BIS winner and the oldest at the time, having won his fourth Best In Show title from the Veterans Class. A third generation Best In Show winner himself, Doodles had sired the Best In Show winning CH Jaclair's Howdy Doody, CD, who had produced the fifth generation Best In Show winner in that line, CH Bannahydes UFO of Beechwood. Impressive credentials indeed!

I weighed the possible match carefully none the less, since the two had very little in common in their pedigrees, similar stock from the same kennel appearing only in the fourth generation behind each. I didn't hesitate long, however. Some lengthy discussions with Huger's breeder and an exchange of pedigrees followed. Finally in early November, Maaca went to visit her 'older man'.

Her eyes were dancing with a devilish "I told you so."

December, 1982

Dear Friends and Family,
   Hello, again. Doesn't seem cold enough to be
nearing Christmas. But it is time to catch you all up
on happenings around here. Mama Jean says I've got

to do it quickly because we're
all going to take off for a
Christmas trip to Georgia to
visit with Granny Kitty. Boy, will
Granny be surprised to see how
big our family has gotten since our last visit. She's
never met my pal Peanut and she's certainly not
going to believe the latest addition to the family.
   Not only do we have a real, live celebrity with a
CH in front of her name [whatever that means] but
the celebrity is going to have some little ones soon -
or so she tells Sable and Peanut and me. All I know
is that instead of a tree and decorations this year,
and a nice box lid with wonderful smells that Peanut
and I like to snuggle into, we now have a playpen
with a sleeping area inside that Peanut and I can't

get into. Sable tries, and he's the most agile of the three of us, but the only one Mama Jean will allow inside is the celebrity.

Maaca has done one thing useful, though. She screamed at that nasty dog with the black head in the window of that house down the street. And it frightened him so badly that he's gone. Didn't help our nerves too much either, but just the same, he's gone. No more head, no more dog! Mom says the people moved away and took him but we think Maaca did it with her scream. Most times, though, she just takes Mom away to shows on weekends and we have to stay home alone and we don't like it much. Of course, sitters come and walk and feed us, but it isn't the same as having Mom here to play.

Well I don't care what Queenie says. I get the front seat on the ride to Georgia. Okay, okay. I'm hurrying. Have a happy holiday and a great new year from all of us to all of you.

Pittypat

Birth of a Prince

Arabelle was a gift from my father-in-law on my thirtieth birthday, a golden 1965 Mustang with two huge doors, and a back seat suitable for two double amputees. The powerful 289 engine had no difficulty with the load on the trip back from Georgia but the interior was overwhelmed by the four crates and the x-pen and supplies needed by the dogs each time we stopped. With Maaca less than a week away from whelping her first litter, we stopped about every two hours. Peanut and Sable were satisfied with having their crate on the back seat of the car. Not Maaca. And not Pittypat. Maaca 'sang' in her high soprano if her crate wasn't sitting in the passenger seat and poor little Pittypat threw up if her crate wasn't in the passenger seat.

Neither the seat belt nor the side mirror visibility would permit both crates to be in the passenger seat at the same time. Every two hours or so, I'd stop, unload the x-pen and set it up with water and a little dry kibble, unload all four dogs, clean up Pittypat's crate and switch the two. Between Maaca singing and Pittypat throwing up, it was a very long trip back from Georgia.

Paw Prints Through The Years

It gave me plenty of time for debating what my next vehicle was going to be, and weighing the tradeoffs of gas consumption against adequate space for my growing family if I decided on getting a used bus to replace Arabelle. If I'd thought I could successfully drive an eighteen-wheeler, I'd have considered trading up to one of those before we finally reached home.

Maaca especially had enjoyed a lot of love, attention, and belly rubs. Puppies' heads or rumps or something round were now very prominent protrusions along both of her sides, and she invited attention and rubs to that area.

The box and whelping area were ready, and I'd read and reread the material on birthing puppies until it was grimy with finger oil. But no book ever tells the whole story. I'd been recording temperatures, but the lowest I'd recorded was still over 100 degrees. By the weekend following our trip, I could no longer feel the puppies. I despaired that she'd somehow aborted them and I'd missed the event. I was kicking myself for having made the Christmas trip with her, fearing the long car ride had somehow hurt her and the puppies. The subject of all my concern seemed content to snooze by my side, or watch me as I puttered around the house doing chores. I certainly had seen no 'nesting behavior' as I understood the term. We were sixty-one days from the first breeding, so I'd already decided to take leave for the next few days to stay close to home.

Sable was especially attentive, bringing her toys in which she showed no interest. Peanut and Pittypat slept and occasionally growled at Sable for bumping into them in his frolics. Finally I dozed off in front of the TV late that Sunday afternoon in the midst of some boring show, then awoke suddenly to realize Maaca was not in the room with us.

My search eventually took me upstairs to find her sitting on the rug of my bedroom licking a tiny, mewing black and white thing which looked like nothing so much as a little mouse. On the dirty bedroom carpet! Within a foot of the open door to the enclosure with the clean paper floor and sterile, towel-lined whelping box! So much for planning!

I left dam and puppy as they were and rushed to connect the heat lamp, warming pad, and to fill the hot water bottle that was ready in the whelping area in the bedroom corner. When I returned there was nothing left for me to do but tie off the cord, weigh the little guy, return the squirming four ounces of puppy to his anxious mom, and try to shift them to the clean and prepared whelping area.

Maaca responded by dropping a second bundle into my hands, his sac still intact. This little one, it turned out, didn't want to breathe, so I thumped and rubbed and slung for what seemed like an eternity before finally being rewarded by some squeaking from the tiny little thing. He weighed in at an even three ounces, and either from birth or probably from my rough handling, he had a huge umbilical hernia. I tried to put a bandage over the protruding hernia and Maaca removed the bandage about as fast as she removed the ties on the umbilical cords. Fortunately, iodine does a wonderful job of sealing things so the ties weren't really needed by this time.

Despite all the confusion, two tiny little boys and their mom settled into their fresh, clean sleeping box. The boys nursed, slept and twitched. I cleaned up, fed the other three dogs and brought them upstairs to the bed where they could watch quietly the new life cuddled close to Maaca in the puppy area. It took all my resolve not to pick up the tiny bundles and caress them. Together they weighed only seven ounces and would fit easily into the palm of one hand.

Peanut was only slightly less fascinated by the puppies than I and would sit or stand at the perimeter of the x-pen balanced on her three legs watching them. Pittypat and Sable sniffed around a bit, climbed on the bed and went to sleep. After a brief growl to establish her authority, Maaca ignored them all and curled contentedly over her babies, accepting offerings of honey-laced food and water at intervals. She would always let me steal one or another of the puppies to hold without complaint or any signs of stress, something which continually impressed and thrilled me.

I was prepared for the fact that puppies are born much less mature than human babies with eyes and ears sealed shut. But I was not prepared for how rapidly they grew. Pink noses seemed to acquire additional black dots in the time I could go downstairs for a cup of coffee and return. I postponed leaving for work each day as long as possible and rushed home in the evening in anticipation of what changes the hours away had wrought.

Because of my first career as an aerospace engineer and my specialty of navigational astronomy, I'd picked a kennel prefix that was the Latin word for star. And I decided to just alter the pronunciation of Maaca to use it as meaning 'maker' instead of 'make a.' So the puppies became Astra's Magic Maaca and Astra's Mischief Maaca. Magic was always the more correct one with larger ears and a finer muzzle. Mischief, the smaller one, was the one whom I worried over, because of his physical problem with the protruding umbilical hernia.

By three weeks the little brats were trying their legs and walking through the uprights of the x-pen, and I was spending nights designing and constructing bumper pads to affix to the pen to keep the puppies inside. The books directed that puppy chow should be offered at about three weeks, because the mother's milk should be declining. So I dutifully mixed honey with puppy chow and puppy formula in a blender and offered it to the babies. It was a slapstick comedy!

First, I had to put Maaca somewhere else, because she'd growl at her puppies and inhale the small dish of puppy must. Left alone with the dish, the boys walked through it, lay and rolled in it, then slowly began to get it into their mouths when they tried to chew on each other's ear or face. Sable, Pittypat and Peanut looked on with fear that I was going crazy as I rocked with laughter at the messy little boys. Mother Maaca always rushed back to the pen at this stage in the boys' lives with heightened interest in giving the boys a complete bath, and cleaning off all the sweet tasting goo from their bodies.

By seven weeks, Sable had developed a definite dislike for the puppies that tumbled after him and tried to bite his tail with tiny, sharp teeth. Pittypat and Peanut had wisely discovered that the seat of the sofa or the bed was the only sane and safe place in the house with two rowdy babies tearing around the floor. I reveled in the sweetness of puppy breath when I held them and basked in the charm of having two tiny heads settle in sleep using my toe as a pillow. Maaca spent brief periods of time with the boys still, mostly fending off their attempts to nurse, nature having provided all the weaning instructions necessary in those tiny needles in the boys' mouths. She rejoined the rest of us on the big bed to sleep at night and her place was taken by a stuffed gray bunny which the boys adored.

Of course, there were constant phone calls asking for one or the other of the boys. And I knew that the time was fast approaching when I should make a decision on letting one of them go to another home. As I watched them romp and tumble with one another over the rugs until they had exhausted themselves, and then drop and sleep around my feet while I watched TV at night, I wished many times that I could slow the passage of time or the progress of their development toward maturity. As ears came up and muzzles lengthened, I speculated on how the two little ones would look as adults, but a part of me wanted their puppyhood to last forever.

Shopping 101

Time marches forward whether we want it to or not. By the puppies' eleven-week birthday I had made the painful decision to let Magic go to another home.

As every woman knows from the time she can see and toddle, shopping is the crutch to get through all times of emotional upheaval. When you're sad, you shop to feel better. When you're happy, you shop to celebrate. The first thing a female learns in the school of life is to find something on which to focus her attention, and her shopping, to deflect emotions. My trouble initially was that I was too sad at the prospect of parting with my dear little puppy to have any desire for an inanimate object of any kind.

But that is what mothers are for. My mother always knew how to push my buttons, but never when to keep her mouth shut. So when I mentioned on the phone that Magic was leaving with his new human the next day, and I might just spend the rest of the day shopping, she immediately said, "Well, I hope you don't buy any more rugs. You've got quite enough in your house already."

Of course, my immediate response was to determine where I could possibly put another rug. I spent the early morning of Magic's last day with me in crying. He was a gentle, quiet little lamb, especially adorable when he tired of play and settled into his favorite sleeping spot at my feet, using my big toe as his pillow. He'd weighed four ounces at birth to Mischief's three, but he grew to be the smaller of the two and promised to be very tiny as an adult. So despite the handicap of the huge umbilical hernia, Mischief was the more correct of the two for show.

Magic and the boys' favorite stuffed toy, Grey Bunny, left together to go to their new forever home. I cried and held my other five close, though holding a hyperactive little puppy that missed his brother and his favorite toy was more a plan than an event. All the while I walked around my house trying to find a spot that 'needed' a rug.

The architect designed the house to be functional and modern, putting a brick entrance way at the front door. It had functioned well for almost twenty years without a rug. But suddenly the most important thing in the world was finding a perfect cover for that spot.

Despite the sadness of parting with little Magic, I was delighted with the extended family we gained and with the soft beige rug I brought home from my shopping trip. Magic's new humans decided to give him the call name of Sunny. In the weeks to come, they frequently called, wrote, and sent pictures to tell me what a wonderful, shining part of their lives he'd become.

Maaca went into the excessive shedding routine typical of dams following the weaning of a litter of puppies. The shedding is often so sudden and so profuse that breeders refer to it as 'blowing coat'. For a while she welcomed the sweaters I covered her in when we went walking in the cold April evenings. The excessive hairs and the human and dog tracks soon turned the soft beige rug into a muddy, furry, spotted mess.

Pittypat and Peanut licked a few of my tears and went back to their routine of sleeping away most of the evenings on the sofa. Sable discovered that Mischief could be a fun partner in romping on the floor, but became more and more jealous when Mischief's developing coordination allowed him to jump up on the sofa seats and into my lap.

That same happy and hyper activity level introduced a danger to Mischief, however, that could not be ignored. The dark shadow of the liver could be seen through the dangerously thin membrane of his hernia, and any one of his risky antics could have ripped the skin, exposing his liver and resulting in his bleeding to death before I could have gotten him to help. So at fourteen weeks, I accepted the advice of my vet to do risky surgery to fix the hernia. Mischief went to surgery in the early morning, a happy, bouncing bundle of energy. When I stopped off after work, I bowed to recommendations not to see him and get him excited. An early morning phone call the next day notified me that he was dying.

When I arrived at the clinic some long anxious minutes and several near traffic accidents later, the staff there brought him to me in an examining room. He was too weak to look at me or even try to wag his little tail. I remained through the day with him held in the circle of my arms, nestled in his baby blanket on the examining table while normal activities of the busy vets' office went on around us. I promised him if he'd just try to live and get better I would never, ever leave him again. Near closing, the doctors told me they needed to take him away for the night, but I gave them two choices: keep me with him all night, or let me take him home.

At home that night, I pushed sofa and love seat together to make a secure nest, banked pillows around the sides and slept with a small, scared puppy resting against my heart, a scratchy incision and stitches helping to keep me sleeping lightly. The four adult dogs seemed to understand the urgency of the situation and quietly settled down to sleep on

31

the floor in the den. Not a single one of the four tried to join me and the struggling puppy in our makeshift nest. By the second day after his surgery, Mischief was improving rapidly. Within a week he would recover his happy, sparkling love of life. I would spend the rest of his life attempting to make up for leaving him alone that night at the vet, in pain and scared, a long lifetime of keeping my promise to him never to leave him again.

He was my first papillon puppy to watch grow into a butterfly. The ugly ducking stage was an eye opener. Legs grew before body hairs filled in, so for a while I had a long-legged, gangling teenager.

He picked the once beige rug in the entranceway as his potty spot when I wasn't attentive. Stains in the thick cotton were hard to get out and I was ready to throw the misshapen thing away. I made the mistake of telling my Mother who replied, "I told you not to get the thing in the first place."

I blame her totally for the fact that it was still on the bricks of the entranceway a week later when I wearily arrived home from work, umbrella in one hand, briefcase in the other, to trip over the edge of the rug and almost fall into the first floor.

Mischief absorbed all his dam could teach him about climbing fences and improvised additional escape tactics on his own. By five months of age he could not be contained in any area that did not include a secure top. What he couldn't scale, he chewed through.

I got the brilliant idea – well, I thought it was brilliant until Mischief showed me the error of my ways – of using baby gates, one on top of the other since he would easily climb over a single gate. He chewed thru the rubber mesh of the bottom gate and got out. I replaced the rubber mesh on the lower gate with wire covered in cloth to keep the rough wire away from puppy skin and mouth. He climbed up the lower gate and chewed through the rubber mesh in the upper gate. I replaced the upper gate's rubber mesh with wire. He climbed both gates and was poised on the top one ready to leap down from the five-foot height when I caught him. I gave up, got a large crate with six sides and confined him to that when I was going out of the house.

I finally moved the grungy rug from the entrance floor to his crate where he never again seemed to think it acceptable as a potty spot. I went out shopping for a new rug for the entrance. This time I picked a fake oriental one with patterns and colors of orange and brown. I refrained from making any mention of this to my mother during our phone conversations.

Mischief began practicing scales and singing at the top of his lungs. Fortunately for my relations with neighbors, his range of singing did not include the extremely high piercing scream favored by his dam. But he was an accomplished 'talker' by the time he turned seven months of age. Ears and eyes were secondary to the language he could achieve with the whines, barks and yodeling sounds he mixed together to communicate.

Eventually I surrendered and left him free in the house. His choice of entertainment during the day sometimes seemed to be heavily weighted toward the investigation of light cords and electrical connectors for televisions and such. After some research I determined that a clear liquid called Bitter Apple was successful in rendering such habits distasteful in the very real sense of the word. So I bought a gallon of the stuff, a small sponge brush and set about painting a layer of the bitter tasting liquid on surfaces I didn't want him to chew. This seemed to keep him out of trouble with the dangerous electrical cords, but he turned his attention to the fringe on the entrance room rug. In no time at all, the rug was denuded of fringe and he began to work on the holes where the fringe had been to unravel the rug.

Jean C. Keating

I refrained from mentioning this latest problem with the entrance rug to my mother. I'm a slow learner, but I do eventually learn.

I did go out once more on my third shopping venture to find the perfect covering for the entranceway. I came home with yet another fake oriental, but one without a visible binding or fringes that an inventive puppy could destroy.

By this time, perhaps Mischief's age was sufficient to end his chewing habits or I was successful in the choice I made. Whatever the reason, the rug now became a warm and cozy spot on which to sleep away the hours while he waited for my return from work or shopping. And for all the rest of his days, he never failed to anticipate my return to the house and to be waiting with wagging tail and smiling face in the entranceway to greet me. When I changed cars, it took him two days to figure out the new motor's distinctive sounds. When I changed decorating styles, the first consideration in choice was the availability of just the right rug for the entrance. I refrained from telling my mother "I told you I needed the rug in the entrance."

All my life, I'd lived with dogs, but one dog at a time. So watching the interaction now among five of them was a delightful education. Pittypat retired more and more to the sofa cushion beside me, and Maaca became the recognized leader of the pack. I don't think she ever told Mischief, however. He always pranced around and acted as if he were running things. Peanut was happy to be a part of the gang. Sable started out being very aggressive with Mischief as he aged, and ended up being on the receiving end of the growing puppy's assertiveness.

Early in Mischief's life, Sable would eat his own dinner and then push Mischief away from the puppy's dish in order to eat a second meal. By seven months, Mischief was picking up his little dish with a growl and bringing it to wherever I was for protection or to show me that it was

34

empty and he wanted more. But the two young males shared a love of toys and one or the other would always initiate a peace treaty by bringing a large toy to the other and shaking it, inviting the other to a tug-the-toy game.

Early December brought the first snow accumulation that Mischief had experienced, since he was too young the previous winter to ever go outdoors. Peanut, Maaca and Pittypat would not go out in the white mess until I dug them a path from the back deck to their exercise area. Sable, like any self-respecting chihuahua, just stood on the back step and shivered. Mischief, now nearing eleven months old, launched himself in a leap into the nearest pile of snow, which was some twelve inches deep since I'd piled the excess from the path I dug on to the existing layer. His surprised yelp as he sank past his ears, brought his protective dam running to help, while I stood in the snow leaning on my snow shovel and laughing hysterically.

It was my turn to cover the office during the holidays, so the gang and I decorated the house for Christmas and stayed close to home. Considering the youth and inquisitiveness of Mischief and Sable, it was amazing that we suffered the loss of only three broken ornaments for the tree, and none of them ended up in someone's stomach. I had more than enough shopping to satisfy my needs with five little dogs in the family. The Christmas letters got out with only a few chew marks to attest to the help offered by my little busybodies.

December, 1983

Dear Friends and Family,

    This holiday season seems a little less hectic than most. I guess it's because we aren't traveling this year. Mama Jean has to work over the holiday  so we're staying close to home. This means that we're again decorating with a tree and everything. I hope that lots of those nice smelling boxes under the tree are mine, because I've been especially good this year trying to keep things running smoothly.

    And let me tell you it isn't getting any easier. Especially now that we've added a new member since last year. He's Maaca's son and he's named Mischief. And that's what he is too. He pulled Mama Jean's favorite little bear off the tree and gutted it- almost pulled the tree over on him. And he doesn't listen to me, or his mother or Sable or anyone. Peanut just wags her tail and tries to keep out of his way. He pulled the toy mouse off the tree a little later, and then tried to eat the butterfly. I hope we don't all get a bad reputation because of him and miss out on all our lovely presents.

Our Granny isn't going to see us this Christmas, but she may be just as glad. We went down to see her in the fall. Maaca even consented to compete in a few shows just so Granny could enjoy the sight. But Granny didn't find the shows to be very interesting. In fact, she was very upset with Mama Jean for talking ugly, said she'd never been allowed to call anyone a bitch. Then Granny got up and insisted on leaving when the show announcer came on the loud speaker to request that pom bitch number 6 pick up her armband. It didn't help that Mama Jean was laughing so hard at her that she couldn't talk and explain about dog shows and the females of my species. Let's just say it was not a resounding success as an outing, and I don't think Granny will be attending any more dog shows. Mama Jean explained it to us later, said the language of dog shows offended Granny's Southern sense of propriety – whatever that means. I guess it means we won't invite her to attend any more shows with us.

We've got lots of presents under the tree and many of them smell just wonderful. I don't think

Mischief deserves any presents this Christmas. He got more than his share back in January when he arrived. Mama Jean went just a bit overboard when he came. He had matching blankets, playpen, towels and even a stuffed Pooh Bear to sleep with. He didn't really appreciate the large stuffed bear, until his little brother Magic went off with their favorite stuffed bunny to another home. Then Mischief started to drag this huge stuffed Pooh Bear everywhere. He even takes it to bed with him and that bear and Mischief intrude too much on my sleeping space. I sure hope he doesn't get any more toys like that for Christmas this year.

Here's wishing you the best of holidays and a happy and healthy new year. Keep in touch. Licks and hugs from the gang and me.

Pittypat

The Potato Chip Syndrome

Anyone who has owned papillons for any length of time will tell you that living with the breed usually produces an ailment called The Potato Chip Syndrome. As in "you can't eat just one." Well, one papillon is so much fun that you tend to want another and another.

By now I knew that I would never be able to let Mischief go off to a show with a handler. The near loss of the little minx had produced a mindset that could not consider ever letting him leave home. So I set about planning my next move to have a dog to show that I might consider allowing him to leave for a week or more, or on long weekends.

First off, I arranged to repeat the breeding of Maaca with Huger hoping to get a little lady like Mischief. Well, maybe not exactly like him. Maybe quieter and more like his brother, Magic.

But this wouldn't be enough, I told myself, because I really needed a mate for Mischief. This comes under excuse #x for adding more papillons to the pack. So I called around, discussed pedigrees, markings, likely size, attributes and all, and finally was lucky enough to be offered a little lady named

Jean C. Keating

Spice. Not wanting to make the four-hour drive alone around the Washington beltway to Silver Spring to get her, I invited my friend Kathy to go along for company. I was about to learn a painful lesson in the willfulness and assertiveness of the papillon nature.

While I wrote the check to adopt the three-month old, Spice crawled up in Kathy's lap, looked my friend in the eye, planted a kiss on her nose and said, "You're mine."

I brought little Spice home after dropping off my friend Kathy at her home in Richmond. Spice cried all the way from Richmond to Williamsburg. At home she sulked. She walked around the ring at classes with her ears down. She spent a good deal of her time in the front entrance expectantly waiting for Kathy to come. I fed, watered, cared for, trained her – or tried to – but it was Kathy she waited day after day to see. Four months could pass between visits from Kathy, but each time Kathy arrived she was greeted with excessive tail wagging, ear waving and dancing feet. Spice ignored my existence as completely as was possible given her need for food, water and exercise daily.

I tried sending Spice to several weekend shows with a handler. The only time she would walk around a show ring with ears up was when Kathy was on the other end of her lead. Fortunately, Mischief had taken a liking to Spice, and she to him. She'd accepted him as a soul mate. So I left Mischief to make Spice feel comfortable, and went looking for another show bitch. Of course, when describing this to my eighty-plus year old Mother, I referred to this as seeking another lady papillon, having finally bowed to the fact that Mother was never going to feel comfortable with the use of the proper doggie term of *bitch.* As long as I avoided a word which to her was *bad language* she would continue the conversation to the point of telling me I was crazy to have six dogs. She would live to question my sanity even more as the numbers increased over the years to come.

Paw Prints Through The Years

My first-loved papillon Vinnie came through again to add charm and excitement to my life. He'd already sired one all champion litter with a daughter of another famous champion, American/Canadian/Bermudian, and International Champion Kra-Li-Mar Czar. I was honored to be picked to get one of their puppies from a repeat breeding. Two months after Spice arrived to shun my attentions and reject my show plans, Vinnie's daughter out of Czaretta [Champion Kra-Li-Mar Czaretta Bow Creek] came to grace my home and life. Her name was Fallon and she brought with her a quiet and loving nature that was as delightful to live with as she was to watch.

Mischief and Sable were beside themselves with two beautiful little girls to impress. Since I still had plans to show Sable, he remained intact, so I began to plan a rearrangement of my house to ensure that Sable didn't get too friendly with these two sweet young things at the wrong time.

Maaca added more excitement to the zoo by delivering two more little boys. I grumbled a bit about not getting a single girl out of two breedings and promptly fell in love with the two little fellows. Unfortunately, the smaller one weighed only two ounces at birth. He was determined but much too small to nurse, try as he might. If he got his mouth open wide enough to get it around a nipple, it was too stretched to produce suction. Fortunately for this little one, who was named Astra's Alpha Axis and dubbed Spinner, both my boss and his dam were very indulgent and cooperative. I converted a lateral file in my office to a puppy bed, took puppies and mother to work with me each day, and regularly milked nourishment into his wide open mouth from his mother's nipple. By two weeks of age, he'd gained sufficient size to nurse on his own, and there was no stopping him after that. His larger brother was named Astra's Amorous Accident and called Rusty. He would become the first home bred champion of the Astra pack.

41

Jean C. Keating

Now I had four puppies at home of varying ages and I couldn't wait to get home at night to enjoy their antics. Mischief still had the run of the house, but the others were secured in a large covered pen during the day for safety. Mischief still met me upon my return at night. But his greetings were as much to hurry the release of the other puppies so they could play as to welcome me home. Mischief and Sable enjoyed the role of big brothers, and began to teach the four younger ones all they knew about escaping out of pens, climbing fences, removing each and every toy out of the toy box and littering the floor of the entire downstairs with their stuffed toys and any stuffing which could be removed from the insides of the toys.

Peanut and Pittypat hurried through outside potty routines and swiftly retreated to the sofa in the den to get out of the way of fast moving bodies and toy destruction activities. Maaca joined them as soon as she could turn over all puppy feeding and training to me. With nine dogs and four intact males in the house, a total rethinking of sleeping and housing arrangements was necessary and I embarked on yet another career, that of Decorating for the Dogs.

Decorating With Dogs

The structure of the house fortunately lent itself to redecorating for the convenience and comfort of the growing pack of canines. With nine active fur children, the bed wouldn't hold us all. I was beginning to suffer from sleep deprivation as a result of the increasingly frequent fusses over territory that Sable and Mischief were prone to have during the night. Mischief generally dragged a big, stuffed bear to the side of the bed, fretting until I assisted him in getting it up on to the bed, since it was far too large for him to get on the bed himself. Pittypat was growing more unhappy with the space taken up by the little ones in what had been, at one time, her private sleeping place. Not only was Mischief prone to defensive posturing over his space, but he also fussed if she came near his stuffed bear. With the addition of four more little people, changes were necessary if any of us were to enjoy our rest.

The architect intended the long room running at right angles to the laundry for a shop and storage area for outside tools. But it made a perfect room for the dogs, so a half door was installed to separate it from the laundry room. Even the

43

inventive Mischief could not climb or chew through the door, though the white paint had to be touched up at least once every six months. Shelves wide enough to safely hold their crates were installed at a convenient height for me to see into, clean, and load with food and water cups and bedding. Higher shelves around the room held clean bedding, medicines, and most importantly, boxes of doggie treats. One end of the long room was covered in papers for a convenient toilet area, but most of the floor area was available for play. The six young ones slept in their crates at night now, although finding a crate large enough for Mischief and his huge stuffed bear challenged the width of the shelf.

The six active little rascals had the room to themselves for play during the workday. Each morning I'd shake out the scatter rugs and place them artistically, to my eyes anyway, about the room for the comfort of the dogs. Each evening I'd find them wadded or crumpled against the wall with a few hunks chewed out and strewn about the floor along with any and all toys that started the morning in the toy basket. The three older girls retired to the TV room for quiet and leisurely pursuits during the day.

The fenced area to the side of the house was very unsatisfactory for nine active dogs, so I called the trusty fence company and outlined my plans to fence the entire back yard. I had hopes that the area would be so vast that even with the nine active little fur-people, I would have some hope of keeping my flowers and azaleas. I still had a lot to learn about gardening with dogs.

The representative from the fence company tried to keep a straight face when he came to write up my order and reduce my brief instructions to the exact specifications needed by the workmen. His face looked a bit more drawn after I brought out Spinner, now a two-pound, six- month old wiggling, hand-and-face licking little bundle of energy.

"Now, the gates need to be so closely fitted to the gate

posts that this little fellow can't get through," I instructed.

"You don't mean to turn that little thing out into the yard, do you?" the man asked hopefully. "He'll be bigger when he goes out into the yard, won't he?"

"He's probably as large right now as he'll ever be," I replied, dashing the man's hope of an easy solution to the fence building. "And I'm certainly going to want him to be able to run in the yard."

I didn't bother to explain that I didn't find the time for evening walks anymore, with so many little faces to feed and look after. Running and playing in the yard was needed to replace our former walking exercises.

Very precise instructions as to extra braces followed. The green, vinyl-covered chain link, that arose almost four feet above the ground, was firmly buried in the dirt all the way around the bottom of the fence and the gates were so secure a gerbil would have found it difficult to get through. The first thing I did after construction was to put the dogs in the yard and go next door and call them. Thankfully, none of them could get through the fence, although Mischief walked right up the chain links and was poised on the top ready to jump down on the other side when I ran back to the fence and caught him.

Contriving a suitable sleeping area during the day for the 'older' girls was a bit more difficult. It was obvious that they could not stay in the 'dog room' as the large space off the laundry room came to be designated. Six young dogs were a bit much to expect Pittypat and Peanut to tolerate, so the den was restyled to make it comfortable and appealing for the two older ladies. Maaca decided she had more in common with the ladies that she had with the puppies, so sleeping platforms had to be designed for these three to rest comfortably on the back of the sofa and against the wall. For Peanut that meant also designing a ramp to allow her to reach the sofa and the back of the sofa in spite of her bad knee. It was a wonderful excuse to give them my old foam pillows and order new down ones for my own bed.

Peanut decided that she liked the den nest so much that she didn't want to make the trip upstairs any more, so a lovely cat bed with quilted panels on all sides and top was added to the love seat in the den as her own private retreat. When the young ones came out in the evening to frolic through the house, it was often crowded on the sofa. But they usually left me a little space upon which to relax and watch my own television, as long as I spent some portion of that time throwing toys for them to retrieve. And nights were certainly more restful for me with only two little lady dogs sharing my bed.

Gardening proved to be a very different challenge now that the dogs had the run of the entire yard. When the gardening books lauded the beauty of butterflies in the garden, they certainly didn't mean the ones I now had in abundance. These little butterflies in fur suits seem to have at least eight legs apiece and all eight were usually engaged in a type of help that any garden would do well without.

Over the years, I'd gradually reclaimed segments of the yard from natural forest floor and planted small, one- gallon azaleas. Hues of pink and mauve mixed with white. With the passage of years and the help of a giant pine tree to replenish the acid content of the soil, the tiny plants had become quasi- trees. Coral Bell azaleas were not supposed to grow more than three feet in height, but the two beside my computer room window didn't read that part of the gardening book. Delaware Valley Whites must have gotten themselves confused with trees, for they were competing with the dogwoods for altitude. Now that I could garden and play with the dogs at the same time, I began to incorporate the two efforts into each outing with the dogs into our newly fenced yard. I busied myself with pruning and cutting back my wildly-growing azaleas, dropping the excess in a steady rain down on little dogs who delighted in helping me by treating the ever growing pile of limbs as new toys. Unfortunately for me, the pruning and consigning of limbs to trash piles were being recorded in active little brains as slightly different scenarios from the way I viewed them.

Papillons are called the most 'cat-like' of all dog breeds. They lick their paws and wash their face like cats, perform heart-stopping leaps on, off and between pieces of furniture in the house and flower pots on the deck, and like cats they sometimes learn from observing what their human does. Often it wasn't what I wanted them to learn.

One of my frustrations with gardening is that all the beautiful pots of flowers that decorate outside decks during spring and summer have no place to go in the fall and winter. There's no place for them inside during the winter, and they die if left outside. So I decided to replace the annuals in one of the large pots with a small azalea, thinking it would weather over and provide greenery on the deck during the winter. Two days later, I discovered that Spinner and Sable had 'pruned' the little plant down to the dirt. When I tried to fuss at them, the look I got plainly said, "We're just doing it the way you did it, Mom." Spice climbed into the pot and made it her outdoor bed as a final negative comment on my efforts.

Planting iris rhizomes was even more difficult. The recommended technique requires digging a wide trough and then raising an elevated ridge down the middle of the trough, so that the rhizome rests on the ridge and the roots can trail down into the two segments of the trough on either side of the ridge. Somehow this procedure seemed to attract a lot of helpful little paws that wanted to rearrange the freshly dug site.

In anticipation of a beautiful future season of irises, I'd carefully chosen a beautiful [and expensive] iris called Syncopation, anticipating the color display of its thirty-eight

Jean C. Keating

inch high blooms with violet purple falls, gold standards and blended tan edges. In my mind's eye I could see them blooming beautifully against the fresh green of dogwoods. As I strained to plant each rhizome on the carefully constructed ridge, I realized that six sets of little puppy paws were doing their best to level the ridges I'd just spent a good hour constructing. I scolded my helpers and started over, being careful to watch more closely and growl at any unwanted diggers. Finally the crew of plant-bed wreckers appeared to go to another section of the yard to play with something else, or so I thought.

When I finally decided to give my back a rest and looked around, Mischief, Rusty and Spinner were playing tug with one of my larger rhizomes, and Sable was guarding three others that the helpful little brats had unearthed almost as fast as I'd planted them. It was hard to get mad at them when I realized that I'd done the planting with bone meal. While that had always been my fertilizer of choice, I had to laugh and repeat ten times to myself that changes were necessary now that there were meddlesome little fur people in the garden.

With the coming of a larger fenced area, gardening now had to include cleanup of many, many little dirty paws in addition to the cleanup of gardening tools.

Though we didn't get to any shows during the fall, we spent plenty of time trying to learn to walk on lead, sleep in our crates at night, and allow some of the plants to remain in the flowerbeds.

December, 1984

Dear Friends and Family,

Gosh, I'm very late with the letter this year. We've already heard from a lot of you. Thanks for all the lovely photographs that you've sent with your  greetings. Got a card and picture from Magic/Sunny. He likes freshly laundered clothes. His Christmas picture showed him settled nicely on top of a basket of linens with a big grin on his face. His family thinks he's the greatest and can do no wrong, so they don't care how many baskets of clean clothes he squashes. He's happy as can be.

The mob around here has certainly increased this year. If you haven't heard from us since last Christmas, you'll be surprised to hear that there are four more of us in the gang this year. You aren't surprised? You know Mama Jean is inclined to be a bit compulsive, do you? Yep! Well Spice came to live with us first. She likes Mischief all right, but she'd rather be in Richmond with our Auntie Kathy who lives in an apartment where they don't allow dogs. Spice says she will not appear in any show ring without her Kathy, and so far has managed to get away with dropping her ears, looking sad, and getting her way.

Then Fallon came to live with us. She's a delight. So gentle and calm. She's very nice to have around after all the rough little boys I've had to put up with. And as if Mischief and Sable weren't enough to deal with, Maaca produced two more little boys. They're named Spinner and Rusty and neither is as pushy as Mischief, but that still makes for 14, or is it 15, more puppy feet running around here. Oh, Mama Jean says I can't multiply, that it's sixteen!

I'm getting on with the letter! I am! I will so get this finished before the new year! Well, here's wishing you a great holiday, what's left of it, and a grand new year.

Pittypat

PS If you have anything to say about it, don't let Mama Jean have any more puppies please. I finally got my bed space back and I want things left the way they are.

Dog Talk

Evenings seemed to pass all too quickly with nine active little personalities to keep happy. You can only spend so much time, however, saying 'good dog' to first one and then the other. Trying to give equal time to each was getting very repetitious. Since I needed more and more time in the evening to fix their dinners or clean up after them as their numbers increased, I mixed verbal conversations with body language to provide them attention. I began just talking to them about anything and everything that happened during the day, or just describing what I was doing. It was apparent that they enjoyed the sound of my voice, and one by one they all expanded their verbal skills and joined in the conversation. Fortunately, Maaca was not a big talker, since her mode of vocal expression was a piercing high soprano that made us all cringe. Spinner's response was a one note alto monotone that he frequently and joyfully injected into the conversation. But he accompanied his vocal input with gravity-defying leaps into the air just for the sheer fun of life. Mischief developed a lengthy vocalization in response to my verbal nonsense, starting with a little bark that went into a growl and ended with a long drawn out yodel. Pittypat's response was mostly a loud pant that sounded more like she was trying to whisper than anything else.

Dear, grateful, little Peanut hugged the corners and the shadows, looking on and weakly wagging her tail, afraid to bark and shatter this cherished but not yet trusted family relationship. I began picking Peanut up in my arms and dancing around like a crazy person, laughing and playing at having fun whenever noise or a coming storm made her react with fear. Living adjacent to the College of William and Mary and five blocks from the restored area of Colonial Williamsburg had it drawbacks. Fireworks were frequent and loud and Peanut already had an unusually strong terror of thunderstorms. Since I couldn't stop either the noise of fireworks or the thunderstorms, I was determined to train the puppies and hopefully Peanut as well that such things were fun, a source of laughter and games instead of something to fear. I was successful with the puppies. Peanut's anxiety attacks to thunderstorms lessened, but never really stopped. But at least fireworks displays from the College or Colonial Williamsburg ceased in time to be anything she or the puppies appeared to even notice.

So with Peanut in my arms and the puppies jumping around my legs, I would walk and skip about the house doing chores in the evening. Fortunately none of my neighbors lived close enough to hear, or I'd have ended up at the funny farm. As time passed, friends got to hear more and more of this dog talk when they phoned, however. Since the phone provided no smell of another person and no sound that could be heard by the dogs, they assumed my side of phone conversations was directed at them and would join in as usual. It made quite a din at my end of the phone. But then most of my human friends are dog people, so they usually laughed it off. I did notice an increased error rate with items ordered out of catalogs however.

Paw Prints Through The Years

It was a hard year by many standards.

I'd hardly had time to put away the Christmas cards and add Magic's Christmas picture to my memory book, when word came from his grieving owners that he was dead. He'd gotten sick over the holidays, been taken to an emergency clinic and given the wrong medication, and had died four days later. In the years to come, many people wanting a puppy would have to pay the price for that careless clinic because the evaluation of available emergency care would become another important consideration in all future evaluations of potential puppy homes. I threw away the bedroom slippers that Magic had used as a pillow before he left for his forever home the year before; they brought tears each time I saw them and remembered the beautiful little dog whose life had ended so early.

Rusty and Fallon grew into beautiful young adults, and were soon off on the show circuit with their handler, chasing points and having fun.

Spinner remained smaller than either his litter mate Rusty or his older brother Mischief, and was only three pounds at eight months of age. He always made me laugh, however. He would run up to me to be picked up, then spin around and position his body with head facing away from me, so that the hand that reached under him and lifted him up always had him positioned so his little head was pointed toward mine for a kiss. I teased him aloud about knowing his name so well and developing a habit to match his name.

He was too tiny to show, but I took him with me when Rusty, Fallon and I went off to the Metropolitan Area Papillon Show in late February. One week later, Spinner developed parvo. Though he'd had all his immunizations, the process didn't seem to give him the protection it should have. The four days struggle to save him utilized all that veterinary science had to offer. It brought him out of the parvo. But as is often the case with this terrible disease that

Jean C. Keating

is a big killer of small puppies and older dogs, his tiny size afforded him too little reserve to survive the struggle and he died of a heart attack.

I grieved for both of these beautiful little puppies, even while I tried to be grateful for ribbons and points which Rusty and Fallon accumulated on their way to becoming Champions. Each in his or her own way was fun to watch in the ring but very different from Maaca.

Rusty could not be trusted to behave in any predictable manner, acting like a showman one day and ignoring judge and handler the next. Fortunately, on one of his good days he attracted the attention of the pet columnist for the local paper. So he became the first of the Astra troupe to be featured in a newspaper story. He cared nothing for the lovely story but enjoyed the liver treat the photographer offered him at the end of their session.

Fallon developed the most beautiful fringes I'd ever had on a papillon, but she lacked Maaca's arrogance and showmanship. She played the demure, shy lady in the ring so many times when judges approached her to view her alertness, that I considered using her growing supply of ribbons to wallpaper or ribbon-paper the TV room in purple and white. Unlike cat shows, where coming in second is awarded some points, the second best in a dog show gets no points and a purple-and-white ribbon. The ribbon says 'Reserve Winner' but I call it the *best-of-the-losers*. I teased her aloud about being the reserve-winning princess of the east coast. She had the looks to be a great show dog but not the desire. So as soon as she got the points to justify the Champion in front of her name, she came home to warm her favorite pillow in the family room when she wasn't following Mischief around the house.

Spice got her wish and was retired from showing without garnering a single point toward a championship. She came home to renew her favorite game of teasing Mischief

54

by taking any and all stuff toys away from him. She never checked the toy box for anything. She'd follow Mischief around, softly yipping in his face until he dropped a toy to yap back, then she'd grab the toy he'd just dropped and run with it. Despite his aggravation with her over his toys, especially a stuffed dragon I'd given him to replace his huge brown bear, there came a time when she was irresistible. Their pedigrees seemed to click, they both were willing, and in June the two produced a single puppy that I named Astra's Brainy Bear and called Bear.

Naturally for this big event in Spice's life, I invited my friend Kathy down to stay for a few days. Between Kathy and I holding the little puppy every chance we got and Spice washing him every five seconds, little Bear grew to be as spoiled and demanding as any only child. He was prone to sleep on his back with four feet sticking up in the air. As he grew bigger, Bear's toys were frequently held in his front paws and above his head as he rolled on his back, a tiny red bear or a yellow duck waving above his head.

Peanut seemed especially fascinated with the little imp, and Spice outdid herself in being protective. For once, Peanut could not be intimidated to back away, and would frequently stand on her three good legs, nose pressed into the side of the playpen as she stared in fascination at the playing puppy. Spice's grumbling seemed to go unheard by either Bear or Peanut. Maaca was delighted to let someone else deal with puppies, and would give Spice, Bear, playpen and Peanut a wide berth on her way into and out of the den.

I wanted a picture of the 'immediate' family together, but every picture of Spice and puppy with Mischief seemed to show a father who was trying to leave the scene. I assumed at the time that Spice was making threats to leave her puppy alone. In the years to come, I would discover that father and son just did not like one another. Being stupid, stubborn, silly or whatever, I would insist on sharing a life with these two strong-willed males for the rest of their days.

Unfortunately, Mischief either taught little Bear all he knew about climbing out of things, or simply passed it to him with his DNA. It took several near heart-stopping incidences to realize that Bear was too smart to really jump down from the top of the four-foot fence around the yard. He delighted in bringing me running to retrieve him from his perch, and would happily bark and wag his tail in glee at having won my undivided attention. Finally I took to ignoring his antics and after a few sharp yips and yaps, he'd climb back down the chain link of the fence as easily as he'd climbed up them. For reasons I never fathomed, my blood pressure always managed to remain out of stroke range during these episodes. Training young puppies as smart and manipulative as little Bear most certainly can be a hazard to your health.

Lights Are Dimming

Through the summer and early fall the puppies perfected their skills at getting into mischief. Peanut acted like a proud and indulgent grandparent, gently wagging her tail when the six young ones tumbled into her bed or crashed into her as they careened about the floor.

Maaca continued her takeover of the pack, and was not reluctant to provide corrections to any and all of the younger six, including Spice. Maaca gave every indication of doubting that her 'daughter-in-law' had sense enough to raise a puppy like Bear, and was as quick to correct Bear and Spice as she was her own three or Sable.

By now, Mischief outweighed Sable by about two pounds, so the places were reversed between the two and Sable was often on the receiving end of jealous posturing. He began to back away from much of the races around the house and retire more and more to the safety of the sofa cushion. He found that if he tried to hug my side, Mischief would come over to grumble, but that a position on the sofa cushion above and behind Maaca was a safe haven.

Papillons are called butterfly dogs because of their big ears, which are feathered, large and carried obliquely to resemble the wing of a butterfly. But anyone who has ever lived with these light-boned, little bundles will tell you that most of them really believe they were meant to fly. As Rusty and Fallon reached their mature size, Spice and Bear's relationship switched from dam and puppy to partners-in-crime, and Mischief attempted to teach them all he knew about climbing. Naturally if you're up at a nice height, the next thing to do is just see if those ears will enable you to fly.

The benches around the fireplace in the living room provided a wonderful ascent route to the kitchen counter top that adjoins the benches. Just about the time I'd get my dinner on a tray and sit down on the sofa in the den to eat, I'd look across the den and into the kitchen to see one or two puppies proudly walking across the counter top in the kitchen, plotting a take-off point for a grand leap to the floor. Before one of the little monkeys broke a leg, I decided that the rug I wanted to buy for the entrance hall would have to wait so I could funnel money into fencing off the living room from the rest of downstairs.

By now the toy box was three times the size of the original one. I spent a lot more time picking up toys from the first floor, as the brood increased in activity and number of toys acquired. It always seems as though it should be possible to train them to put their toys back into their toy box, but I was never enough of a trainer to do that. I spent too much time laughing at them and getting the necessary shots and stuff that I even forgot the simplest rules about getting them comfortable with car rides.

On Bear's third trip to the vet, he experienced a bout of motion sickness. It made me realize that I'd never taken him on any drives except on trips to the vet. So for many evenings thereafter we made short rides to the drive-thru chicken and hamburger places to associate car rides with fun things instead of shots.

Pittypat seemed to get quieter as the activity level

around the house got more frantic. She still ate with zest, but she seemed to sleep more and more and to lose weight despite the food consumed. She was only a little over eight years old. I suspected nothing serious but wanted to be sure, so a routine blood screen was done as a part of an exam. The shocking diagnosis was that she was suffering from an autoimmune disease, her body treating her red blood cells as invaders and killing them off. She got extra treats to compensate her for all the medication she had to take, and was glad to let me carry her up and down the stairs to her bed at night. She delegated any chores as alarm barker and guest greeter to Maaca and Peanut, the later of whom was diligent enough at sentry duty for any three dogs. Despite her fatigue, she never lost her sunny disposition around the hard playing youngsters.

We decided to decorate another tree for Christmas at year's end. None of the pack contested Pittypat's right to nest in the lid from the decorations box while the rest of us clowned around with tree trimming. When it came time to add the skirt to the tree, we found that Pittypat had made it into a pillow, so we spread a white towel around the bottom of the tree and put the presents on the towel, leaving her to snuggle with the brightly decorated tree skirt as long as she wanted.

Peanut greeted the Christmas fireworks calmly. She danced around on her three good legs and began to show some signs of trying to play with Bear, who'd fascinated her since his birth.

Spice was as aloof as ever. She wanted Kathy to come, but Kathy was busy with a new job and a new boy friend.

Mischief developed a new habit of racing at top speed toward me when called, then stopping at the final minute to stand on his back legs, lift his front paws up and wait to be picked up. He seemed to think this was especially funny when he had just grabbed the ornament I was reaching for to put on the tree.

59

Rusty found the bows on the presents much more fun as toys than the stuffed animal ornaments, and would run off with a bow and refuse to return it.

Fallon and Maaca quietly observed all the action from a comfortable spot on the sofa, two demure champions who could not possibly think of behaving with such unseemly and unladylike manners.

Sable chose a favorite stuffed frog and succeeded in getting it to the pillow on the sofa behind Maaca to enjoy peacefully, confident that the ruling alpha female would not let Mischief bother him.

In the soft beauty of Christmas lights we settled in for the holidays to wrap up another year of challenges met and fun shared by us all.

December, 1985

Dear Friends and Family,

Holiday greetings from Williamsburg and the gang. I've taken over the responsibility for the

Christmas letter this year, because Pittypat is feeling too tired to write just now. In fact we're not going to try to make a trip to Georgia this year to visit our Granny because Pittypat is recovering from surgery to remove her gall bladder.

Hope you've all been healthy and enjoying a great year. My son Rusty got his championship this year to become the first home bred champion to carry the Astra prefix. We had a lovely party for him, with a three *A* theme, since he is now Champion Astra's Amorous Accident. Don't tell Mama Jean I said this, but she is hopeless at baking and the cake didn't look a thing like an *A*.

Then Fallon finished her championship a little later in the year. And I'm now a granny myself, since my son Mischief and this flighty little witch named Spice produced a lovely little scamp named Bear. I'm not too thrilled with my daughter-in-law, but hopefully her haughty attitude about the show ring won't rub off on my grandson.

Mama Jean went off to England to a dog show in the spring, and Mischief is still fussing because she left us, and especially him, at home. She's tried to explain about quarantines or some such, but we're not buying any of it. I'm sure I could have collected some beautiful ribbons to add to my collection if she'd just taken me along. On the other hand, someone had to stay home and keep this crowd on the straight and narrow. I don't allow a lot of scrapping and fussing, especially when Mama Jean is trying to snooze on the sofa.

Now that we're getting so many of my relatives, sons and a grandson around here that all have names beginning with Astra, Mom has taken to calling us the Astra gang. I'm the one in charge, but don't tell Jean. She thinks she running the show, and its better if I let her go on thinking that, at least until I can figure out how to operate the can opener and the car.

Hope the holidays bring you everything you want. I want that red velour pillow I found at the pet store. I was very annoyed when we left the store without it.

Best wishes for the new year from me, Pittypat, Peanut, Sable and the rest of the Astra gang.

Maaca

Champion Debonair Maaca Choice

Best Laid Plans

The new year brought additional staff and responsibilities in my professional life and I began to bring more and more work home to complete at night. Such behavior did not go unnoticed or unpunished by the small, furry members of my family and resulted in many spin-offs of the 'dog ate my homework' stories.

I made plans to breed two of the girls. In Fallon's case, I owed her breeder a puppy back sired by the male of her breeder's choice. In Maaca's case, a beautiful Canadian best-in-show had come to visit at just the right time and I was still trying to get a little girl from Maaca to carry on her blood lines. Spice and Mischief took advantage of my distraction to conspire between them to produce a third litter.

I busied myself re-arranging three bedrooms to put a play pen in each for dam and puppies. Of course, I had to also decide on another two themes to use for the two additional puppy rooms. All right I admit it; I'm just a bit compulsive with the puppies. Each dam had to have her own matched set of baby stuff. Maaca 'owned' the Pooh Bear set, retaining squatters' rights to it from her first two litters. I found a beautiful set with blue and pink ponies on bedding, blankets and playpen for little Spice along with two small and cuddly stuffed ponies for pillows. Fallon got a new set with colorful balloons and alphabet blocks in primary colors. I was busy, having fun decorating for the three big events.

So my excuse for not correctly analyzing the strangeness of one telephone conversation with my mother was simply mental overload. Communications were often strained in the early months of the year because I'd refused to make the drive to Georgia over Christmas. I'm certain all mothers take a course called Guilt 101 in which they learn just which buttons to push to make their offspring feel the most guilt at not doing whatever said mothers think they should do. Twenty-two hours on the road at Christmas had been out of the question with Pittypat. Since my Mother wouldn't drive and wouldn't let me send her airline tickets or train tickets, she'd spent the holidays alone. By some law that was never a part of my college physics classes, it was always a great deal longer to travel from her house to mine and back than to travel from my house to hers and back, at least to hear my mother tell it! Our phone conversations had come to be infused with subtle attempts at guilt laying. In defense, I had become extremely obtuse.

She began this particular phone call with a tale of a robbery at her home. When I pressed for details of what was missing, she said that 'someone' had broken in and exchanged her TV set for one that looked the same but didn't work. This had followed months of stories about thefts of baskets of lace or a single knife or a favorite frying pan. She wanted me to 'do something with the police' because they wouldn't come out to take a report anymore. Such were, I knew, growing signs that she was getting older: losing things, refusing to accept responsibility for losing them, and seeking to blame it on theft. The mental image I was running of this story had me trying to talk and not choke with laughter as I imagined a thief climbing over her locked

65

gate with an identical TV [never mind how this little fact would be known to said thief] balanced in one hand so he can exchange it for the 'good one' in her house. I tried a logical approach with her, which only made her madder, because neither I nor the police would take her seriously, so she hung up on me. Instead of getting a book and beginning to read up on Alzheimer, I had a good laugh and went back to readying the house for three litters of little papillons.

Little Bear began and finished his show career by following his grandmother's example and finishing in five short weeks. Poor little baby. He didn't even get a first-birthday party in his honor. Pittypat worsened despite the dramatic measure of removing her gall bladder. That procedure sometimes buys a dog two years of life. Sadly it gained us only a few months. Blood transfusions bought us only a brief span of days in which she came back home to be held and loved and to say goodbye.

The phone call that came the morning of Pittypat's death seemed like insult added to injury at first. I had offered to foster one of several papillons rescued from a puppy mill. The caller asked me to meet her at a dog show in Richmond to pick up a little girl named Twinkle. I wanted to scream and cry, tell them I just lost my best friend. But somewhere from my past, the words of my father's counsel came clear and strong: when God closes a door, he opens a window. I briefly settled on a time and location to meet at the show and hung up before returning to my crying.

During the hour drive to the show, I adjusted my attitude to reflect the realization that I could do nothing better for Pittypat's memory than give Twinkle a better life. Fortune seemed to smile on that attitude, for I found a parking spot right at the door to the show site and arrived in time to watch the long-coat chihuahuas being shown. I was especially fond of one tiny, fawn-colored male that was about the size of an eight-week old papillon puppy. I had seen the dog and owner at other shows earlier in the year and thought the little dog was adorable. His owner and handler was a very tall and large footed male who moved with grace and elegance outside the ring, but who minced and stumbled-footed around the ring with his tiny partner. Tiny Stevie took his class, and the mismatched pair came out of the ring in time for me to congratulation them. The owner expressed his embarrassment at stumbling over his dog in the ring and said the dog was just too tiny for them to make a smooth partnership.

"Just let me know if you ever decide to sell him, because I'd love to have him as a pillow decoration", I responded, before rushing off to find Twinkle. Within an hour I had collected the shy and fragile little Twinkle and had gotten a history of her current feeding schedule. In my present depressed state, I had no interest in relieving the vendors of doggie things I usually thought I couldn't do without, and I was on my way to the exit when Stevie's owner stopped me.

"If you still want this little male, he's yours," he said.

Now there I stood, with my mouth open. I'd just taken on the responsibility of an emotionally scarred waif, and now I was offered a tiny little fellow that was the size of a puppy, a full-grown dog that would never get to be three pounds! Moreover, I was an hour's drive from home and didn't have an extra crate in the car with me. But I'd just told this man an hour before, "If you ever decide..."

The owner explained that he and Stevie had not only lost their bid for points in dogs but that he'd almost fallen over the tiny performer. "You may not have noticed, but my feet are longer than Stevie," he added.

I struggled with an appropriate reply. It would have been hard not to notice, because the owner/handler's shoes were polished to a bright shine rarely seen in show rings other than the evening formal scenes of Westminster. But I didn't want to come off sounding as if I thought his feet were too big for him.

"How much do you want for him?" I stammered in confused indecision.

"Nothing," he responded. "We have several mutual friends, and I've checked you out in the last hour. Just give him a good home."

I don't think my eyes were the only ones tearing as his big hands tenderly placed the tiny fawn bundle into my arms. He turned quickly and left before I could confirm that his cheeks were as wet as my own.

Twinkle made the trip to Williamsburg in her crate on the front seat beside me, fearfully crouched down into the new sleeping ring I'd gotten for her at the show. Thank Detroit for power steering, because I drove with one hand all the way while I talked constantly to the frightened dog. Stevie slept the entire trip, held tightly against my shoulder by my other arm.

Mischief took the addition of two new fur-people with more grace than I had expected. Although Stevie was around two years old at that time and intact, he did not seem to generate the jealousy in Mischief that others, especially Bear, did.

Yard time had to be arranged to provide Twinkle with a special fenced area for herself. Never having known grass in the puppy mill, where dogs are sometimes born, live and die in little wire crates, she regarded the green stuff with suspicion and some fear. The pushing and butt sniffing in which the remainder of the pack wanted to engage was terrifying also, so she spent her first few weeks protected by an x-pen until grass and new brothers and sisters ceased to terrify her. Steps she could not then, and never did, learn to traverse.

Stevie blended in with the pack immediately. His first afternoon in the house, he stood on the living room rug in the center of the pack, his tail wagging a greeting, while he touched noses with first one and then another of the larger dogs. He had to be carried into the yard, because his short legs couldn't negotiate the stairs any more than Twinkle, but once on the ground in the yard, he sprinted through the grass trying to keep up with the larger papillons. He'd run until he got tired, then sit down wherever his headlong dash had taken him and wait for me to come and pick him up.

Twinkle found it hard to adjust to being loose in the house. The energetic romping of the pack was too much for her to take, and even Peanut's gentle attentions were rejected. It was tiny Stevie who finally convinced her to share a doggie bed with him in the evenings and enabled her to become a part of the growing pack of happy little people in keeping me company while I watched TV in the evenings.

Despite the addition of Twinkle and Stevie, Pittypat's loss was still a painful memory when Fallon produced her first litter, a beautiful little girl we dubbed Dixieland Delight. She would later go back to Fallon's breeder and become CH Caress of Bow Creek.

Spice produced one tiny three-ounce girl, so perfect and petite that she could have been called nothing else but Elegant Elf. It took three days to determine that she would be a red sable like her sire, Mischief. Spice cleaned her so constantly she stayed wet all the time. When Elf had not gained any weight at three days, another trip to our favorite vet determined that the little miss had the nursing instinct a bit confused. She insisted on putting her tongue against the roof of her mouth and the nipple under her tongue. The amount of suction obtainable in that manner is nil, zero, zip!!

My fine motor skills were severely challenged as I tried to hold a Lilliputian head in my big hand, force a tongue that was about half the size of my small fingernail down from the roof of a tiny mouth, transfer said tongue and mouth to a nipple without breaking a jaw or losing my hold while the owner of said nipple did her best to continually lick my hand and the puppy's face. I was never so glad in my life to get to the three-week old puppy mush stage of growth.

Maaca had produced her first two litters on the sixty-first day from the first breeding. In so doing, the second of her two puppies each time had been premature. I was determined not to have that problem again, so I arranged for her to be bred only once. By day sixty-four, when she made no attempt to birth the large puppy revealed by x-ray, I arranged for the delivery by cesarean section. And as luck would have it, the local paper was doing a story on the vet's office, so Maaca got her picture in the paper as she was being prepped for surgery. She didn't look a bit distressed. In fact, I would swear that she was glaring at the photographer, probably demanding to know why he hadn't given her a ribbon for her performance.

Over the years, I've discovered that life with papillons has some constant points of amusement. One is the cautions always issued by my vet that the dog will 'probably be groggy' from the anesthesia when I bring him or her home, and that I shouldn't be worried. After rocking the crate all the way home in eagerness to get out, said dog usually bounds out through the crate door when released in the house and then races around the dining room table with me in fearful pursuit trying to explain that said butterfly is supposed to be groggy. Maaca was no exception. I did manage to catch her just seconds before she made a spectacular leap up the side and into the playpen where I had foolishly placed her puppy before releasing her from her crate.

Since I now had three litters of one puppy each, I had the brilliant idea that I'd put them in first one and then the other playpen so that they could learn to get along with siblings. The mother dogs had other ideas. Fallon wasn't interested in caring for her own puppy, much less the other two. Maaca would have nothing to do with strange puppies in her kingdom. Spice was the only one who would allow all three near her, and her frantic attempts to keep the three clean left them no time to nurse or play.

The presence of three litters in three different rooms in the house produced a lot of laughs. Peanut couldn't decide which room to visit first with three puppy playpens to entertain her. Sable and Mischief stayed in constant squabbles without Maaca downstairs to keep order. Either Bear or Rusty, probably both, discovered that walls could be chewed and managed to destroy a nice chunk of the corner of the den before I spoiled their efforts with some bitter apple.

All too soon, three months of laughing, cleaning, feeding, and cuddling puppies passed and it was time to let them go. Caress went home to Fallon's first mom, in fulfillment of the agreement long ago when Fallon had come to join the Astra gang. By agreement she would never carry the Astra prefix but be named Caress of Bow Creek, adding the Champion in front of her name in short order.

Maaca's son was named Famous Footsteps, and called Fraph. He had his famous father's flowing coat, but a solid black head. The lack of noseband and blaze would have seriously faulted him in the show ring, but was no detraction from the joy he brought a friend in Ashland who started out only wanting a lap warmer. Then she got intrigued with his background and ended up showing him for a while. They went as far as winning the two major shows needed to become a champion and acquiring fourteen of the fifteen points he needed. Then the little stinker decided he didn't want to show anymore, and Fraph and his doting human gave up the show ring for the comfort of the sofa.

Little Elf went to Maryland to become the favorite bed companion of an elderly lady. Elf never grew to more than four pounds and her new human had to have a special set of stairs made and carpeted just so the little darling could come and go on the bed without human assistance.

Spice, Maaca and Fallon resumed their positions in the pack. I was grateful that my quiet boss bitch dog was back in charge to keep the scrappy little boys from chewing on each others' ears and my walls. I returned to working on the computer and to fielding complaints from my mother of phantom burglars.

I Could Have Told You That

Last week's headlines screamed out the news that "dogs are smarter than previously believed." I hope this startling revelation didn't cost me too many of my tax dollars. Paying a bunch of 'behaviorists' some hundreds of thousands of monetary tokens to conclude what most of us pet owners could have told them for free does not impress me.

I certainly would have gladly informed anyone who'd listen that dogs think, reason and act on their reasoning. Indeed, it seems to me that dogs' only exhibited stupidity is in putting up with the arrogance of human pronouncements of superiority based on the tiresome 'we build fires and have a spoken language' dodge.

Dogs recognize human speech as well as animal communications. And they read body languages and thoughts as well. If you think not, just try to find one when you're planning a trip to the vet, or get out of the house alone when you're going to the drive-through chicken place. And I've yet to hear of a dog that destroyed 300,000 acres of forest by starting a fire.

I already suspected that dogs thought things through and planned their responses accordingly, long before I met little three-month old Spice. Years ago, Maaca had convinced me that the soft flowing fur and large butterfly ears covered an active, reasoning and sometimes manipulative brain. After Elf's birth, I began to seriously consider what to do about Spice's unhappiness.

She had made up her mind from the day I bought her that she wanted to live with my friend Kathy. So Kathy and I consulted on Spice's future, and concluded that a change of lifestyle was necessary – Kathy's. Kathy sublet her apartment that prohibited pets and rented a small house where she could welcome Spice to live with her. Spice walked away from my home and my life – she'd never been a part of it anyway in her way of thinking – with head and ears held high, 'smiling' at her Kathy all the way. I could almost 'hear' the reassuring dialogue, "I forgive you for taking so long to take me home, I know you've been busy."

When Spice decided that she and Kathy needed to increase their family, she picked out a beautiful 125 pound German shepherd dog [GSD] – who was already bonded to a reasonable looking and behaving human male – and proceeded to court them both. Two years later, Kathy married the reasonable looking human and Spice got her family complete with loveable and tractable Dutch, the GSD. Christmas pictures were a hoot with Spice attempting to mother and direct her blended family in seating arrangements.

Dutch and Spice ate from bowls set side by side, the tiny dish of the papillon and the huge bowl of the GSD looking almost comical in comparison. Each behaved with perfect table manners, avoiding any intrusion into the other one's dish.

Then in his twelfth year, Dutch became ill with a slow-moving cancer. He lost interest in eating and would often leave his food untouched in his big bowl. On her own, Spice developed her own means of encouraging her friend Dutch to eat. She would go to his bowl and extract a single piece of his food from the dish, carry it a few inches from the bowl in a line between dish and wherever Dutch was lying and drop it, then go to Dutch and lick his face. If Dutch remained where he was lying, she'd go back to the dish, get a second piece of food, and bring the second piece a few inches past the first piece in the line toward Dutch and drop it, returning to Dutch to again lick his face.

Toward the end of his life, Spice often spent the better part of an hour laying a food trail between Dutch and his bowl, each piece of the trail accompanied by her encouragement to the sick dog to get up and eat. For more than a year, it was her efforts more than anything else that would finally achieve a response from Dutch to eat his way along the trail of food back to his dish.

No one taught her this behavior. She developed it on her own, as an attempt to help her aging, ill friend. The behavior stopped the night Dutch died. Though his food dish remained down and full of food for a few days after his death because no one had thought to empty it, Spice never again found reason to touch the food in that dish.

I don't need a government grant and 'behaviorists' to tell me dogs are capable of thinking and reasoning, capable of far more than learned 'Pavlovian' responses! Just watching and crediting them with the examples of their reasoning power would tell any of us that.

Spice's Kathy sends Christmas pictures still. They seem a bit empty without Dutch. I wonder what Spice is planning next by way of getting another dog into her family.

The Post Hole Affair

Bear's overdue birthday party and championship celebration seemed a happy way to overcome the emptiness of the house after the departure of Caress, Elf and Fraph. It was still in the planning stages, however, when a phone call from my mother's attorney in Georgia postponed the festivities again. Bear was very understanding and just went back to grumping with his sire about territorial rights to the middle cushion on the sofa.

I foolishly thought I could deal with the Georgia crisis quickly, so I left the dogs with a house sitter and flew down to Atlanta. The final seventy-two miles to my mother's home from the airport took only slightly more than double the time spent in flying to Atlanta. Still, this method saved three hours over driving. And sitting on a plane enabled me to begin my crash course in dealing with the care of an aging parent.

When I met with the attorney the next day, it was hard to keep a totally straight face as she outlined the problem. Somehow my mother had convinced a fence company that her fence should be moved to take in a wedge of a neighbor's

76

driveway. Partway through the job, the fence company realized they might be on shaky legal ground and quit, leaving seven fence-post holes across the neighbor's driveway. The neighbor came home after a weekend trip and fell in one of the holes. Neighbor had consulted her own lawyer, asking that Mother pay to repair the holes, after trying unsuccessfully to discuss this with my mother.

This brought my mother's attorney into the picture, and she'd had little success at explaining to my mother that Mother didn't hold title to the wedge of property by county records. Mother 'remembered' that she did. The next time the neighbor went off to work, Mother went on the 'disputed property' and cut down bushes planted by the neighbor.

In frustration, the neighbor was calling my mother's attorney saying she just wanted to discuss this reasonably; she didn't want to fight with "the old woman." Unfortunately, legal ethics prevent an attorney from talking directly with the other attorney's client. But I wasn't bound by any such ethics, so I was dragged in to be the communication link.

I did my best. My long distance phone conversations with the dogs each night were more productive than my day job of trying to reason with Mother while I had the neighbor's driveway repaired and convinced the neighbor that cutting privet hedge had in no way destroyed it. I gave myself a pat on the back for not trying to tell her that privet was a weed that I often tried to kill, generally with no success.

I missed the happy kisses and wagging tails of my canine family that usually soothed away the day's stresses and warmed my return from work. You know you're a dog addict when you start waking up at night because there's no furry body on the pillow beside you.

By the time I worked through the problems and returned home, two weeks had passed. After my return, Mother called each night to complain about some new problem, and to whine that no one would take her part. My desk at work was festooned with urgent notes that generally required taking work home to finish, since my staff had all gone as far as they cared to on this or that project without consultation and further direction. And the gang at home demanded my undivided attention.

Little Twinkle was especially affected by my being away for two weeks. Sometimes during the frantic weeks of raising the previous three litters of singleton papillon puppies, she had been spayed and given extensive dental work. Despite rotten teeth and numerous internal lesions the surgery had gone smoothly and she was physically healthy, free of infections, and finally putting on weight. But the lack of special attention during evenings and weekends that I'd been able to provide after she came to live with the Astra gang had been interrupted. House and dog sitters worked fine for the rest of the self-assured bunch, but little Twinkle had again retreated to the far corner behind the sofa and would not join her newly accepted friend Stevie in the doggie bed at my feet.

Just how to make her future life more enjoyable and less of a strain for her was much on my mind the Saturday after my return home. The weather alone made the day difficult. It was rainy and even self-confident papillons do not like to go out in the rain. I'd spent the best part of an hour in the yard under an umbrella trying to entice the little rascals out to potty. Twinkle acted as though the wet grass was dripping in acid. I finally gave up and brought the gang in, setting out piddle pads and hoping any messes would land on the pads and not my floors.

My first impression of the caller who interrupted my first cup of coffee to ask about a puppy was not positive. I didn't have puppies anyway, Caress, Elf and Fraph all having gone to new homes. But more to the point, I am never impressed with conversations that begin with a tale that the caller can't afford to pay much for a puppy. Dogs, like children, are responsibilities that require allotments of disposable income. They're worth it. They give back priceless love, warmth, and a sense of belonging. But they require money to support. If the very first thing of importance to an individual is cost, then it raises my anxiety level about proper veterinary care and preventative shots being provided to the dog or withheld due to financial concerns.

This caller went on to redeem herself by explaining that she wanted to be certain she understood the needs of papillons for food, veterinary care and support, exercise and more and to be certain that she now could afford to provide a proper home for a dog. An obvious strain came through in the caller's voice when I inquired as to her family makeup, explaining, as I usually did, that small children are NOT the best companions for small dogs. Papillons do happily play with well-behaved children, but since every family always thinks their children are well behaved, I don't bother with self-qualifications of children's behavior.

The caller explained that her husband and only child had been killed by a drunk driver some months before, and that she was alone. She wanted a little dog for company, if she could satisfy herself that she could afford to get and care for one properly. She had been reading up on papillons and thought one might make a perfect companion. I suggested she drive down and meet some, explaining that I didn't have a puppy but if she still felt the same after meeting my papillons, I would try and help her find one elsewhere.

Her visit was a delight for us both. She found the Astra pack to be all her book research had led her to expect from papillons. And to my great surprise, little Twinkle actually came out of her corner and over to the visitor to be petted. As the afternoon visit wore on, it seemed that my visitor and Twinkle sensed in each other the pain of loss and hardship that they shared, and each found solace in the other's company.

Jean C. Keating

It took a few weeks and some soul searching on both our parts to overcome a major concern with the number of stairs in the visitor's home, but some three weeks later Twinkle moved to Richmond to become an only dog. Bear finally got his birthday party in October. So we made it an early Halloween party instead. All the treats contained liver in some form or another. Bear didn't much care what else I put in the mix as long as it smelled like his favorite food. Since he'd usually pick out the liver and eat too much with the resulting messy problem for me to clean off him, the floor, and his crate, I devised some interesting recipes.

Liver simmered in water and garlic was used to cook the rice. And rice from such a mix smelled like liver and was acceptable to the birthday boy. So we had a mixture of rice and liver with heavy smells of garlic and he devoured it like it was straight liver. He usually didn't much care for ground beef, but ground chuck thrown into the mixture smelled like liver too, so he ate it with relish.

We didn't invite anyone outside our immediate pack. Mischief seemed to miss Spice a little, but it didn't stop his consuming his share of the party food. Sable was most indignant that he was expected to wear a party hat and kept tossing it into his dish. Stevie gloried in being the inside of a tiny pumpkin; he could lounge and show off at the same time. Rusty wanted to show me how smart he was, so he kept rolling on the floor until he could reach the Velcro strip that secured a decorative belly band of his Indian suit and pulling it off. Maaca seemed not to mind her costume since she was dressed as a queen, a role that she played her whole life. Peanut considered the entire proceedings a threat to her happy home and refused to move even to get to the food dish. Maybe I shouldn't have tried to dress her as a rabbit.

Fallon was eating for more than herself by the time of Bear's birthday party. She and Mischief were expecting some little ones in December. For the first time I had to step in and settle disputes between Fallon and the other little ones over food. Mischief might have been responsible for her condition, but he didn't feel like contributing his share of the party food to satisfy Fallon's appetite, so he'd grasp the edge of the bowl in his mouth, try to growl at Fallon and drag the food bowl toward me at the same time. Usually this left a trail of spilled food along the floor. The house and floor smelled of garlic and liver for days and I vowed to hold future birthday parties out of doors.

The evening the neighbor in Georgia called to ask for my help again had not been a great day. I'd had a long and unproductive meeting with the state personnel office attempting to get an upgrade for one of my staff. My confidence as a negotiator was in the toilet. The neighbor wanted me to talk to my mother about being so difficult, to make her understand how unreasonable she was being in calling the police to complain that the neighbor's lawn sprinkler was wetting her fence and causing it to rust. I managed to keep calm on the phone, but invented a few curse words when I got off.

Never, never underestimate the dedication of papillons to analyze a situation and try to fix it. One alone will work diligently at a project. A pack of them can move the world.

Since dogs perceive neither smell nor sound when you're holding a phone to your ear, you must be talking to them if you're talking into the phone. If you're upset with the phone, you must be upset with them. All I accomplished with my fussing and fuming was to get the entire pack distressed. Poor little Peanut looked especially crushed. I spent extra time telling them what good little fur-bunnies they were and vowing not to lose my temper again in their hearing.

The next evening the phone didn't interrupt our play or our dinner or our TV time at all. It was two days before I discovered that my dedicated canine crew had chewed through the phone cord and disabled the source of the earlier night's irritation. I refrained from using any nasty words when I replaced the disabled set with a new one. I didn't want to give the wrecking crew any ideas about needing to destroy this replacement set.

By Thanksgiving, we had three beautiful additions to the family for which to be grateful. Both Fallon and I had been through the routine before, so we were able to relax and enjoy the three healthy puppies that joined our lives. The girls were named Halfa Halo and Happy Habit. The single little boy was heavily marked with a solid black head and was named Hardly Holy. I settled back to enjoy the trio and to marvel at the different personalities as they developed. With the previous threesome, the differences in personalities were easily explained by their different parents. The three H's were littermates but grew to be very different little fur-people.

Halo was the troublemaker. Like her sire, she'd climb out of or tear through most barriers to get to wherever she wanted to be, usually defined as where you didn't put her. Happy was Peanut's favorite, because she seemed so confident and quiet from her first days out of the playpen. Holy was the serious, thoughtful, eager-to-please delight. He never aroused the sense of competition in Mischief that Bear had done; he got along with all the rest of the pack without ever seeming to have to defend himself.

I'd used up most of my leave making the trip to Georgia to settle the post-hole crisis as it had come to be identified in my mind. So it was a relief to have a good reason not to venture from home over the holidays. With the small ones just beginning to learn to eat puppy mush, we settled for a few lights and cards to friends, but decided against a tree for the year's festivities. I didn't need the stuffing out of my tree decorations mixed in with the puppy mush, and I was recording a destruction rate of about five ornaments a year by this time. Bear, Mischief and Rusty had become proficient and very competitive in their game to steal and destroy the most little stuffed animals before I could catch them. Besides I couldn't face the sight of the tree skirt that served as Pittypat's bed last Christmas or the empty box lid in which she loved to play.

In spite of the antics of three small puppies and the joy they brought to all around them, I found the holidays a little lonely without my dear, gentle Pittypat.

A Christmas card with a picture of Twinkle was a wonderful lift to my holiday depression. Twinkle was surrounded by toys and seemed to radiate a sparkle that matched her name.

The first of many Christmas pictures over the years came from Caress. She was sitting with her new family beside a beautiful red poinsettia. Her note to the Astra gang said she was delighted to be living with her grandmother and great uncle and that her new family was pleased that she'd begun her show career with a two-point win at her first event.

Fraph sent a large show picture with his Christmas note. He'd managed to surprise even his new mom with his maturity in the ring, but proved to have a very determined steak about having his teeth brushed twice a week.

Sadly, I never heard any more from little Elf, except for brief conversations in phone calls I made to her new family and follow-up checks with her new vet. Her new family seemed never to understand that the Astra pack might have loved her too and wanted to know how she was doing. During the phone calls I learned that she never did grow large enough to get into her owners' bed. So they'd gotten a special set of padded steps for her use in getting on and off the bed. This and other stories of her life gave me comfort that she was loved and cherished, even if I never saw pictures of how she matured.

Holy and Bear

December, 1986

Dear Friends and Family,

I think it is trying to snow. At least it is so cold outside that staying out long isn't an option for avoiding the confusion in this house. And believe me  it has turned into a zoo. We're staying close to home this year because Mama Jean couldn't possibly figure out how to load our growing family into anything short of a sixteen-wheeler.

The tiny little boy who came to live with us in the spring has now taken over the pillow I like to sleep on in the big bed. Twinkle came to live with us briefly but then moved to Richmond. Her Christmas present and note made the pack leader a bit moist in the eyes. But she seems very attached to her new owner, gets carried up and down stairs when she wants to.

We lost Pittypat in early spring, but got a tiny little boy chihuahua at the same time. His name is

Stevie and he's very entertaining. He is very small, doesn't take up any room, isn't pushy like some relatives I could name. I even let him share my pillow on the big bed at night.

I have three of the cutest grandchildren you could ever want. In fact I hope someone, anyone, wants them. They simply will not leave my feet alone when I'm trying to walk across the floor, and they are so ill mannered as to think that my tail is an enticing toy. I've tried complaining to the pack leader, but she seems to think they are funny and won't listen to me. Neither will their dam, that silly daughter-in-law of mine. Maybe I can add my wish to Santa for a new home for the brats. None of the rest of the gang seems to care, but it's my tail they keep attacking.

The older members of the pack and I are appealing to Santa for a new set of stairs to the second floor. The current one isn't wide enough to accommodate our growing population. Except for Peanut and the three young ones, we all have to accompany our human as she goes back and forth to the second floor. Just why everything she wants at night has to be on the other floor, I'm not able to explain. But she seems to make a number of trips up and down the stairs, and the six of us have to fulfill our companion duties by following behind. Sometimes she starts back down before all six of us can get up, and that's the problem with the stairs. They're not wide enough. Mischief is usually in the lead and turns around to come back down before Fallon and I can get upstairs. The resulting gridlock on the stairs is causing a lot of ruffled feelings.

Indeed, I was most indignant the other day when Mischief stepped on my head on his way back down the stairs as I was making my dignified ascent. I would have snapped at him, but you know that queens don't behave in such a manner.

Caress's new human sent a lovely Christmas picture of her and her new family. Mama Jean showed us the picture and explained that the other fur-people in the picture were Fallon's mother and two brothers. Fallon seemed over-impressed with herself when Mama Jean also told her that her daughter Caress had already earned a point toward her title.

We also got a cute note from Fraph. Of course, he has wonderful manners and fulfills his obligations to keep in touch with his first family. After all, he was raised by me. But we have not heard from either Spice or Elf. I knew that scamp Spice was spending too much time cleaning and not nearly enough teaching the basics to her little girl.

Granny isn't coming to visit this Christmas. She said it was just too far to travel from Georgia, and doesn't understand why we don't drive down instead. Granny also explained that since our human wasn't coming and bringing us, she'd taken care of the insurance man herself. He just kept raising the cost of insurance, so she cancelled the policy. Mama Jean didn't seem too pleased with this last bit of information. I'm not sure why, but we're all doing out best to give her extra licks and head butts to tell her we care.

Mama Jean says I have to start licking the envelope flaps now. Queens don't like glue, so I'll see if I can't get Rusty to do that chore. He likes anything.

Best wishes for the new year from the Astra pack and me.

Maaca

Champion Debonair Maaca Choice

Labels

I was delighted to be chosen to attend a weeklong management institute sponsored by the Commonwealth of Virginia. But that delight diminished as the time for departure grew closer. I wanted very much to attend the seminar, but I wasn't at all happy about leaving my little fur family for seven nights.

"Well," say I, "if you don't like the game, change the rules! Little did I realize how much my life was going to change.

The conference hotel was more than willing to let me bring a little dog with me and worked out the arrangements for me to pay the pet deposit separately. Tiny, two-pound Stevie and big brother, six-pound Mischief went along. Arabelle, the Mustang, was loaded so deeply that half the windows were obscured with two crates, a week's supply of casual and professional clothes for me, a week's supply of clean bedding, plastic floor liners for the x-pen, the pen, the ice chest with dog food, cleaning supplies and towels for the dogs and enough plastic garbage bags to keep us organized. Once again, I reminded myself that I really needed to consider trading Arabelle in on a van or a bus.

Jean C. Keating

The cleaning staff commented on the dogs' perfect manners and asked if they'd been debarked. I refrained from responding with horror, although I felt like doing so. I simply explained that due to his tiny size, Stevie had never learned to bark and Mischief had been trained not to do so.

Stevie was very appreciative that the accommodations I arranged in our room included an electric heating pad under his little bed to counter the air conditioning. He and I never did see things the same when it came to the desirable temperatures of rooms. Walking Mischief three times a day gave me a little exercise after sitting in lectures and workshops during days and evenings, and it was very nice to have some of the gang for company during the long week of training.

Training efforts focused on understanding and working with different personalities. Prior to the seminar all participants had been evaluated utilizing a personality scale known as Myers-Briggs Type Indicators or **MBTI**. The **MBTI**, based on Jung's theory of psychological types, measures an individual's preferences on four scales. Each of the four scales represents two opposite approaches to dealing with life. In a simplistic view this means all people can be divided in one of sixteen types and the training was to educate us attendees on how these personality types react to work situations and to each other.

The night before the training sessions began, conference attendees met briefly to introduce ourselves to each other and to receive large buttons proclaiming the results of our MBTI test. I absolutely refused to pin the large button proclaiming my **INTJ** status on my jacket. For all I knew the dratted button meant I was an insensitive nincompoop and a total jerk.

I was too tired from loading and unloading my numerous travel supplies and companions into and out of a tiny car to have much interest in the get-acquainted cocktail

Paw Prints Through The Years

party that followed, so I retreated to my room. Stevie and Mischief didn't take kindly to being separated from me in a strange place, so after a short walk with Mischief, the three of us piled into bed with my book. I may have gotten through three pages before I turned the light out.

I'd pulled the light-retardant curtains, so none of us realized it was light outside, and we all overslept the next morning. Rushing to take Mischief for his walk, feeding and watering the boys, and then cleaning their pen of Stevie's mess took longer than I'd estimated. These morning chores left me barely enough time to get to the opening session. I arrived with hands that were a bit sticky, since Stevie always had to have his morning dosage of Neutra-Cal to provide his little body with the nutrients that his small digestive track couldn't adequately support.

The session began with a presentation and exercise to help us understand preferences. The instructor explained that everyone has a preference in how to do or view a particular thing or area. An individual's preference is used without thinking. The act comes naturally, and is always easier to use than one's non-preferred attribute. Individuals can and do utilize their non-dominant preferences, but usually not equally well. One has to consciously think about it and often finds it frustrating. Right hands, for right-handed people, represent your dominant preference. But right-handed people can and do use their left hand.

Our first exercise for the morning was to write our name with our dominant hand. Then we were directed to repeat this signature with our non-dominant hand. In addition to requiring my total concentration to forming a 'J' without looking dyslexic, I had to constantly unstick the paper from my Neutra-Cal flavored fingers. With or without the additional problem of sticky fingers, it was an illuminating introduction to the energy expended, both physical and mental, in exercising a non-dominant preference.

91

Jean C. Keating

The first of the four scales which Jung used to describe an individual's psychological makeup was the EI scale, signifying Extraversion and Introversion respectively, and defining where an individual prefers to focus his or her attention. The test results labeled me an I or introvert. I argued that I couldn't possibly be introverted since my job required me to work with and speak before large groups of people and I enjoyed doing it.

Not so, the team of instructors responded. They reminded me that I could and had signed my name with my non-preferred hand. I concluded they had not been watching the sticky job I'd made of that chore.

The instructors patiently explained that the big difference between these two types of personalities is the way in which they refresh their energy. Extroverts draw energy from the crowds around them; introverts renew by solitary pastimes, like reading and playing computer games. I began to wonder who had my home under surveillance and observed all those Mastermind games I played before going to bed.

The first day of classes and workshops was followed by another dinner for the entire group and a gab session. I left as soon as I could, returned to my room to feed the boys, and took Mischief for another walk. After calling the sitter to assure myself that the rest of the Astra gang was fine, I explained to Stevie and Mischief that I'd found I was introverted and not insensitive. They didn't seem to care one way or the other. That's the wonderful thing about dogs. They love us no matter what our faults. But they were overjoyed when I announced that we were all going to bed with my book to recharge my batteries. I was asleep before turning three pages; both my glasses and the lights were still on.

Just as well. Since the room never got dark, Mischief had me up at 5:00 am and we were out walking in a grey morning heavy with humidity. Mischief's spotted the little kitten among the pile of lounge chairs and lunged to the fullest reach of his leash before I even saw the tiny bundle of golden fur. I'd started to pull him back before the mother cat bolted out of hiding to protect her precious baby, and I quickly gathered him up in my arms to prevent his finding out just how sharp mother cat's claws could be.

Later, I came back and made friends with mama. I discovered that she had five kittens carefully sheltered among the folded and stacked lounge chairs around the swimming pool, and got some of the dining room staff to give me a dish of milk and some meat scraps to take to the little family. Gossip around the hotel held that someone had dropped the mama cat off and she'd delivered the kittens about eight weeks before. Said gossip mill also held that 'everyone' fed them. I made sure they had breakfast, just in case 'everyone' had forgotten.

I managed to get to the seminar early and with freshly washed hands. We tackled the second set of preferences, those relating to how an individual acquires information. As usual, the more that I heard the less I understood. The second scale is defined as the **SN** scale, with **S** indicating sensing and **N** representing intuition. Sensing types tend to work with a given, deal with the realities of a situation. Intuitive thinkers look to essential patterns, to the relationships and possibilities of situations.

Lunch was self serve, and I got a lot of comments on the amount of meat I put on my plate for my sandwich. Actually, I had in mind feeding two little dogs and some little kittens with most of it. I rushed through lunch after putting most of the meat into a plastic baggie in my purse.

In spite of a side trip to feed the canines and felines, I was the first one back for the informative afternoon session, which gave us all a lot of laughs. The instructors seated participants at tables according to their scores on the sensing/intuition scale. Ask to describe a simple cup sitting in the middle of the table, the different groups showed a marked difference in perceptions. My table of **N** or intuitive personalities called the cup "A Hat for a Leprechaun", "A container for my coke," and "one-half of child's walkie-talkie". The table of **S** or sensing personalities described the cup as 'a paper cup that is green on the outside and white on the inside" and "a cylinder that is open at one end, closed at the other, with the closed end being slightly smaller in diameter."

Well, I could just guess which one an attorney and judge would not want to deal with in a witness box!

When I returned to my room that evening, I was happy to tell my two canine room mates that my large INTJ button didn't stand for insensitive nincompoop, just an inventive nut. I'd spent the day being taught to value the different personality preferences, so when I took Mischief for a walk and encountered the little kittens again, I started to have dangerously imaginative thoughts. Thoughts like, kittens mixed with puppies just might be interesting, the kittens need homes so why don't we take one back with us. Given that these trains of thoughts and the resulting events were all the fault of the Commonwealth of Virginia for subjecting me to such training, I've never understood why they refused to accept the resulting explosion in my family as valid dependents on my state taxes.

The beginnings of these radical ideas were churning around in my head as my roomies and I settled in to bed for the night and watched the latest weather tracks of Hurricane Hugo, which was cruising up the east coast. Mischief gave me a few extra ear kisses in sympathy for my anxiety over the weather report. Stevie snuggled under the cover for comfort. My last thoughts before going to sleep were concern for Mama Cat and her five little ones who were somewhere outside around the pool of the hotel exposed to the elements that were worsening as this major storm moved toward Virginia.

Paw Prints Through The Years

The next days' struggles to understand different management techniques exhibited by **TF** preferences, signifying thinking and feeling, were even more strained by the worsening weather news. I found myself really out of sorts with all the excuses made by the **F** contingent with some workshop examples of an employee who was not producing and finally blurted, "I think Employee A is making a sap out of you all. You should bring the person in, have a talk with him, and tell him to produce or get out." Just how annoying do you think I could really have been if I were, well, extroverted and liked to talk in public!

I always did say my favorite motto was, "God, give me patience and I want it right now! "

The patience and feeling I didn't have for the theoretical personnel in the workshop examples were reserved for finding the homes for the kittens. That evening I was successful in getting three people to take one kitten each, and I brought the other two into my room to join Stevie and Mischief for the evening. Mama Cat could not be found or I'd have had her in the room also.

The last day of the conference was devoted to the examination of the **JP** personality pairs, judging and perception. In spite of worsening weather news, the sessions were informative and productive. What came home to me loud and clear was the worth of having both on a team, because the preferences brought balance to a project. In their extremes, **J** types want to bring things to closure and may make decisions too quickly, while extreme **P** types don't want to make decisions at all because doing so involves eliminating options. It was obvious that my **J** type was in control as I frantically tried to solve the problem of what to do with the two remaining kittens before the conference ended early due to Hurricane Hugo.

In the end, I bundled the two into Mischief's crate, left him free in the car and drove the five of us home to

Jean C. Keating

Williamsburg to see what the rest of the Astra gang would make of the addition of two felines to our little zoo. I had finally figured out what the **INTJ** button stood for: an **I**mpossibly **N**aïve and **T**rusting **J**ughead.

War Zone

Despite growing problems with an aging parent, who seemed to sink deeper into dementia of an unknown nature, I enjoyed the antics of the two tiny kittens. My vet pronounced them to be only about half the age I'd been told by the hotel and put them on formula administered with a doll bottle. My papillon bitches supervised my efforts at feeding and cleanup, convinced I couldn't do it on my own.

My own mother was unable to comprehend the fascination the kittens held for me, being concerned only with ranting about break-ins in her house or fighting with her neighbors. I shared my wonderment and delight of these new-to-me creatures with my Mom, my dear ex-mother-in-law, who was always a friend and confidante despite my divorce from her son so many years before. Mom had been owned by cats in her childhood and we laughed together at my shock the first time the little felines decided to walk along the second-floor balcony rail high over the first-floor living room.

The younger puppies found the kittens fun playmates, but learned quickly not to corner them for fear of sharp little claws. My second trip to the vet with the little cuties had the doctor and his assistant rolling on the floor laughing - mostly at me. By now the yellow-and-white male answered, if only in my mind, to Sunny. The black-and-white one was distinguished in my conversations as Misty, although she rarely answered to anything. Both were doing what kittens do best, batting and scratching at the hands and fingers of the vet and his assistant.

No," I kept telling them. "No biting."

My words were reinforced by slight taps on pink noses. All of which brought no change in behavior from my tiny felines and more amused chuckles from my vet.

"Have you ever owned a cat before?" my vet managed despite suppressed laughter.

"No," I admitted, chagrined that it was that obvious, as I attempted to make another correction to a tiny paw scratching at my hand.

"Well, maybe I'd better explain." The vet made a valiant attempt to wipe the grin off his face as he instructed, "Cats don't, you see, recognize anything like 'No' or 'Nada' or any instruction with regard to them doing other than what they want. They're not going to behave like your puppies. They don't care whether they please you or not."

"Well," say I, determined not to put up with what, to a confirmed dog lover, was unacceptable behavior, "don't tell them they're cats. We'll just tell them they're puppies."

Never missing a breath, my vet pulled the long fringe in each ear of the nearest kitten outward, gave me a mock serious look and replied, "Funniest papillon I've ever seen."

From that defining moment on, I never looked back. I raised two bundles with retractable claws to be a twelve-pound and a nineteen-pound, long-bodied, confident, and sometimes-obedient companions. They came when called because each grew to understand I'd close the door and leave them alone in rooms if they didn't. They played with the dogs as equals and partners because the dogs wouldn't have it any other way.

The months following the addition of kittens to the zoo were punctuated by numerous long trips to Georgia in futile attempts to diagnose and determine treatment for my mother's growing paranoia and roller-coaster emotional behavior. Each time I'd be away for four or five days, I'd return to find the pack had developed some new game.

On one such return, I discovered Rusty and Sunny had started sleeping side by side on the rug in front of the television. It was easy to watch them instead of the far less entertaining junk on the screen. Sunny would usually rouse from rest first, turn his back to Rusty, and back into the young dog's face. Rusty would get up, stretch, and then begin biting at the hairs along Sunny's back. At first, I thought the smarty cat had somehow trained Rusty to scratch his back. But then I realized Rusty was actually pulling at the various clumps of hair he was mouthing. Finally Rusty got a nice hold and really snatched hard on Sunny's back hairs. Sunny whirled and lunged for Rusty, who took off running. I was about to jump in to protect my much smaller dog, when I realized that Sunny's claws had been retracted when he'd swiped at the dog, and his lips had covered his teeth in the mock bite he'd made. By this time, the cat is chasing the dog around the dining room table, on to the living room sofa, along the back of the sofa and down the other side. Finally Rusty stopped, let Sunny catch him, and then turned around and started chasing the cat. Sunny retraced the same path backwards, never once taking the obvious escape route of jumping on to the table or the kitchen counters which would have been too tall for Rusty to reach. By the time the two tired of the game and returned to collapse on the rug in front of the television, I was teary-eyed from laughing and I'd long since forgotten

Jean C. Keating

what I'd been watching on the tube. Apparently the remainder of the pack had grown accustomed to such behavior, because none of them shifted from their own resting positions during these "Sunny and Rusty shows." It was certainly a delightful distraction from the looming problems with my mother.

I finally settled the problem of traveling with my zoo and bought a used station wagon to give me more room for crates. Naturally the car had to have a name, so I dubbed it Bluebelle. But by now the size of the fur-family had grown to the point that it was impossible to house them adequately when I was away from home. So I reluctantly screened and hired a reliable pet and house sitter. Mischief was another story, however. I'd made him a promise when he was so weak after his hernia operation, and I tried whenever possible to keep that promise to never leave him.

The kittens grew to be very large cats. Mischief became more and more frustrated in his attempts to convince the cats of his pack-leadership position, refusing to accept that cats don't recognize packs. Mischief seemed to have watched too many television shows of lion packs, envisioning himself in the role of the lead lion. Sunny had different ideas.

I think they were both just as glad for a break when I packed Mischief into Bluebelle and made the long drives to Georgia. Although the trips never seemed to lead to any useful solutions with regard to Mother, Mischief and I had plenty of quiet times together. Mostly he slept and I drove, but for lack of anything else to do, I chatted away the long eighteen hours of driving. I've always figured some of the language got through to him, because more than any other of my dogs he always seemed to know what I was saying.

Suddenly, Happy, Halo and Holy were beautiful young adults. Holy was my favorite for show, although he

100

demonstrated the stupidity of ever thinking you could predict color markings in puppies from studying those of the parents. Both Mischief and Fallon had wide, white blazes that had been the basis of my worries that their puppies would have white markings on the ears, considered a disqualification from showing in a papillon. Holy was heavily marked with black covering his entire back, neck and head with only a crisp, white noseband to accent his beautifully formed head, muzzle and stop, the sharp and abrupt change from head to muzzle. He appeared in shows sporadically over the next two years. Some shows he won easily, because he was tiny, moved beautifully and had his dam's thick, long flowing fringes. At others, he was dumped because of his heavy markings.

His beautiful eyes seemed to take on a worrying look each time he lost, as though he thought he'd done something wrong. In spite of all the praise and encouragement I could give, I didn't think he enjoyed showing very much, so I brought him home and we went looking for a wife for him.

It took a while to find just the right female, because she had to have a respectable pedigree and be show potential in quality. Despite the fact that I'd had very little success in predicting markings from Holy's parents, I still felt his mate should be very lightly marked to offset his heavy color markings. And, most importantly, the little lady's breeder had to be willing to part with her.

Meanwhile the search was complicated by growing frustrations with dealing with an aging parent. My mother didn't want to leave her home, but imagined robbers at every turn. She took to putting multiple locks on all the inside doors, tiny affairs that wouldn't have stopped a determined intruder, but were very dangerous for a frail lady in case of a fire. Friends and neighbors bombarded me with

Jean C. Keating

stories that it took twenty minutes for my mother to get into or out of the house because of all the keys and locks involved in her chosen security efforts. Naturally each caller had his or her own opinion of how I should handle the situation. I had a security system installed which did nothing to diminish the locks my mother continued to install but increased the phone calls from Georgia as the security system people called to complain that Mother could not be trusted to turn off the system when she went out or came in, resulting in false alarms.

Life was rushed with too much to do and too little time in which to do it. With little forethought, I decided to try a match between Fallon and Bear. It produced two healthy little boys who added more fun to my life but deepen the feud between Bear and Mischief. One of the boys had such a wide blaze that he resembled a Panda bear, so I named him Ivory Illusion. The other was smaller and always the leader in tearing their toys to bits, so I named him Irresistible Imp. It was a naming I often regretted, since the limited times I entered Imp in conformation shows, I misspelled 'irresistible' about two out of every three times on the application. Although Imp won one of the two major shows required among other things to attain a championship, I was too distracted to finish him. Ivory mostly hung around the pack observing the constant bickering that went on between his sire and grand-sire.

The years ran together. The Astra pack and I forgot about Christmas or cards or communicating with family and friends. Finally Mother decided that she just had to move to Virginia because "her friends wouldn't help her anymore." Her plan was to move in with me since she had two dogs and a cat of her own and no apartment would take her with all those animals. I proved that I had retained something from the Myers-Briggs training, and thought through the

Vinne

Great Hair Day

The Queen

A Chip Off The Old Block

Gardener's Helper

Decisions, Decisions, Decisions!

Here's One More

This Salad Needs Dressing

The Devil Made Me Do It?

Do What With This Ball?

Happy Days

situation carefully before acting. Knowing that I could not concentrate on a career and run an office that was more than fifty miles from my home each day and simultaneously worry about what Mother might be doing to my fur family, I wisely decided to buy another home in Williamsburg for her and her three four-legged friends.

I juggled an administrative job that involved the development and implementation of a student data system for reporting by eighty-seven very diverse institutions of higher education with trying to act as sole caretaker for an increasingly angry and demanding problem parent. I'd stumble home in the late evening after a long day of work and early evening chores to find a little fur family waiting patiently with wagging tails and smiling faces. When I settled in the den for the evening, Peanut would snuggle close on the sofa, asking to be brushed. I marveled at the changes good food and a loving home had wrought. Her short black hair was sleek and shining and she'd lean into the soft brush that I always kept on the table beside the den sofa for easy use. She never really learned to like having her nails clipped, but it was accepted as the price of getting a gentle brushing.

Even Maaca began to drop her aloof stance, and snuggle closer from her elevated position on the back of the sofa to brush my hair with her muzzle in support. Bear and Mischief seemed to understand the strain in my life and for a few years declared an uneasy truce. I replaced the coffee table in the den with a glass top supported by four crates. Bear selected the one closest to my feet when I was settled in to watch television. Bear could lie half in and half out of his crate with his head on my foot while I sat and relaxed and Mischief could claim his unchallenged territory on the sofa and ignore Bear's presence.

Misty, the smaller feline, proved to be fastidious about cleaning herself. Sunny, the male, proved to be a slob in his early years. His coat was matted and unkempt and my vet got more chuckles at my frequent visits with Sunny in attempts to determine illnesses that didn't exist. Sunny was just a slob of a teenager. I started grooming him like a papillon. He liked the attention, hated the electric clippers, but objected strongly when the comb pulled on a mat. He was inclined to growl and snap his tail, all of which got him no sympathy and a few extra squirts of grooming spray. He knew better than to bite me; he tried it once and I proved I could growl louder than he. When a few bites at the comb didn't stop my pulling out the mats, he wisely resigned himself at two years of age to doing his own grooming. From then on, he presented himself as a sleek, shiny, golden tabby.

Papillons are talkers and will whoo-whoo — a combination howl that goes into a bark and may end with a whine — to beg for treats. Sunny's purr was too soft to compete with the dogs' vocalizations for attention, so he started coughing. The first few times he positioned himself in the middle of my desk and coughed, I suspected hair balls and prepared for the worst. He had to bat the can of cat treats off my desk's shelf and cough in my face before I got the hint. Thereafter nightly routines generally included the dogs whoo-whooing for treats and Sunny coughing to signal he wanted his share. Misty would let her brother do all the 'undignified stuff' to beg the treats, and then run in at the last minute to join in on the distribution phase.

Dealing with my mother drained my energies. Early on she was sweet to my face, but bad-mouthed me to anyone who would listen behind my back. Doctors shook their heads, suggested I might benefit from support groups for Alzheimer's sufferers, but refused to commit themselves to a diagnosis of Alzheimer's. As the months wore on, she came to fuss more and more to my face. Attempts of individuals in her church to help usually resulted in more difficulties for me. I'd moved her from an old home built at the end of the nineteenth century to a modern rancher with all the modern conveniences like air conditioning and central heat controlled by a thermostat. She never could understand the workings of the thermostat.

One helpful individual in her church responded to her complaints at being too hard up to pay the fuel bill – she wasn't – by indicating she should keep the thermostat set at 70 degrees or below to save money. Being cold natured, she wanted the house to be around 80 degrees. This brought on a constant litany of complaints that the furnace or the thermostat was broken because she was always cold. Would she turn the thermostat up? No. She needed to save money. I needed to "fix" the furnace so she could set it at seventy and save money but have the house warm enough to suit her wishes. I had to laugh to keep from crying.

Finally my search for a mate for Holy brought a delightful little girl named Minerva to join the family. She was very lightly marked with bright eyes and a sweet disposition. Holy hated her. His sisters found her to be a wonderful playmate and the girls had no end of fun pulling Holy's tail and romping with the rest of the gang. Mother grumbled on about my always finding room for a dog when she wasn't welcome to live with me. The Astra gang gathered close on the sofa at night when I finally got home from work and the extra chores needed or invented by my mother. Their constant and uncomplaining devotion and their funny antics kept me going when things were the worst.

Somehow the years slipped away with too much to do and too little time to do it. Dementia created problems for which there seemed to be no solutions and depression ate away at my energies. Dear little Peanut seemed always to be alert to my tiredness and tears, sitting with her body pressed tightly against mine on the sofa or in the bed. And then one night, she collapsed. An emergency vet visit and rushed blood work showed all blood analysis indicators to be off the scale. The diagnosis was an internal cancer that had ruptured. How long it might have been there was impossible to determine. She'd eaten happily right up until the night she collapsed, and a routine check-up only months before had shown nothing wrong. All I could do was hold her lovingly while she was given a shot to gently ease her passing and bathe her face in my tears that she could no longer feel. Somewhere in the back of my head, a crazy little voice said, "At least it won't matter if we get a bad thunderstorm now."

Afterwards I raged at myself, trying desperately to remember if there was some sign of her illness that I'd missed, something I should have done or could have done that I didn't. The stages of grief are predictable and necessary, a payment for the richness of being touched by the devotion of a dog's faithfulness and unwavering love. Knowing that still doesn't make the losing any easier. I never knew her exact age when she came to live with me. The vets guessed at eight, maybe ten years. She and I had eleven years together, of love and caring and peace, except for the thunderstorms. The time with a beloved dog is never long enough.

Minerva grew to be a delightful young lady and with the arrival of her third season, I decided to try a mating with Holy. After all, the reason for adding her to the Astra gang was to have offspring from my beautiful but heavily marked boy, and to hopefully enter those puppies in conformation shows, if and when I could ever find the time left over from work and dealing with my mother. Holy had other ideas. He

106

absolutely and totally refused to have anything to do with her. Imp and Ivory volunteered their services but I refused their help at first. Either one was as lightly marked at Minerva. While I admitted to having failed to anticipate the appearance of a heavily marked puppy like Holy to two wide-blazed parents like Fallon and Mischief, I thought it would be a terrible idea to let Minerva mate with a lightly marked male. But then what do I know.

I finally decided to give Ivory a try and the two produced three perfectly marked babies who were named Jingle Jangles, Jumping Jack, and Justa Joy. Jack went to live in Washington DC and changed his name to Marty. Joy went to Virginia Beach to assume responsibilities for bossing her own household. They called her Precious and threatened to wreck a grooming shop that shaved her ear fringe by mistake. Beautiful little Jingles stayed with the Astra pack to become the bane of her grandfather Bear's existence with her favorite pastime of pulling his tail.

After a fourth season in which Holy repeated his disdainful response to Minerva, I resolved to have her spayed and get on with my life. But fortunately for me and for the future of my Astra gang, problems with my mother intervened and I didn't act on that resolve.

As is often the case, dementia led to failure to eat or to take medicines properly and eventually dictated moving my mother to a retirement apartment. Hot meals were available in the dining room and help was available 24/7 with the push of a call button. Maid service for the apartment was furnished weekly and heavy laundry was handled by the staff. Mother hated it. She'd agree with me one day that something or another could be discarded as we downsized from house to apartment and scream at me the next day for throwing her 'stuff' away. She spent most of her time complaining to the other residents that I'd taken her home away from her, or fussing at the staff that they were ruining her linens by washing them too much. When she wasn't chewing on my ear about some complaint, the management was complaining to me about her making the other residents feel badly with her carping. It was not a happy time for either of us.

One particularly stressful day I returned home to find my dogs in different rooms and crates than where I'd left them that morning. A note from my mother informed me that she'd had a friend bring her by my house and she'd let the dogs out for me. And by the way, 'Jingles and Bear were going to be parents at some time in the future.' Sure enough I found my fourteen-month Jingles, who was in her second heat cycle, smugly curled in a big crate with Bear, her grandfather. That morning, I'd left them in separate crates in separate rooms.

It was not a breeding I would have undertaken because both were very lightly marked. Nor was Jingles old enough to be exposed to the stress of having a litter, if I'd had a choice. After my crying fit, I called a lock-smith and paid him overtime fees to have all the locks in the house changed so that no old keys that my mother might have hidden away would work. The results of this unplanned mating was a delightful little boy, beautifully marked and with plenty of color pigment.. Shows you what I know about predicting color patterns in papillons! But during his seventh week of life, his inexperienced dam snapped at him, bit his tail and damaged it so that it had to be docked. So Local Legend, called Laddie, joined the family, and though he had the 'ears like a butterfly' of all papillons, he fell a little short in the 'tail like a squirrel' department.

Through it all, my little fur-people and my dearest friend and ex-mother-in-law, my Mom, kept me laughing and feeling loved. By now, Mom was nearing ninety, was frail and suffering from a host of physical problems, but her mind and wit were sharp. We were on one of our long phone calls the night I realized Sunny the cat had taught the young dogs to chase the balls that went off the side of the television screen. Mom and I laughed hysterically while Sunny and three dogs pushed and shoved each other in their attempts to get behind the TV. I had it turned to a football game. The pass went off the side of the screen and the fur-children went around behind the TV looking for the ball. With tears washing my face and laughter making my sides hurt, I had to marvel at these little fur bundles who sometimes knew instinctively that their antics were the best medicine for anything that ailed one.

I Believe

I don't know why grown people have so much trouble believing in Santa Claus. I've met him twice and I can assure you that he does exist.

All right! So the first time I just thought he was a fat little old man dressed in a Santa suit. He'd offered his time and the time of his wife to support the local humane society. The fundraiser allowed people with dogs to have their pictures taken with Santa and his wife.

I'd decided that if I didn't get out Christmas cards soon to friends and family they would forget who I was. I now had six generations of papillons in the house, although Laddie was very young and Maaca was fighting a host of medical problems. So I decided that I needed to make time to have a photograph made of at least five of the six generations and use the photo of the event to prod my energies into sending Christmas cards before the dogs forgot how to write.

Santa and his wife were decked out in the prerequisite red-and-white suits, sitting in front of a beautifully decorated Christmas tree. I recognized the item from Christmases long past, thought it had been more years than I wanted to admit since I'd put one up at my house. Mr. and Mrs. Claus showed the dewy signs of too much clothing for the heat generated by bright camera lights trained on their persons. I arrived with five of my gang: Maaca, Mischief, Bear, Ivory and Jingles.

Santa never batted a thick white eyelash or raised either of his bushy brows at the sight of five small dogs entangled about the legs of their inept handler. Maaca was calm and self-assured as always. Her son Mischief was fretting and trying to boss the other four, also as usual. Mischief's son Bear was poised to push his position if an opportunity arose. Bear's son Ivory was bounding from one direction to another, trying to go somewhere, anywhere. Ivory's little daughter Jingles was too intimidated by being out with the older pack members to do more than flatten herself against my shoulder and try to hide under my chin.

"Do you want five separate pictures?" Santa asked.

"Oh, no," I stammered as I tried to pry Jingles off my shoulder. "I'd like them all together in just one picture. "

A bushy white brow elevated a little in surprise, but I hurriedly added, "Maybe you could hold some, and Mrs. Claus could hold the rest."

Only one of the five dogs wore anything resembling a Christmas outfit. Mischief was wearing a short-sleeved cotton tee with Christmas decorations and words emblazoned across the back proclaiming his usual motto about life: "I want EVERYTHING." My Christmas-picture Santa probably thought this little shirt had been donned for the picture. It really covered the scars of Mischief's battle with a shar-pei some five months before.

"Well, we can't have the rest of the family slighted for Christmas finery," Santa said. "Let's see. Who would like this little hat?"

The conjurer pulled a tiny red hat with a white pom-pom at the tip and a small chinstrap out of his fat sleeves and offered it to Maaca. With all her six plus pounds of regal

Jean C. Keating

disdain, Maaca ducked her head and gave him a look that should have frozen the sweat drops off his face. She did consent to settling comfortably against Santa's right hand as I took the offending hat away.

"Maybe Bear will wear it," I suggested with a nervous laugh, as I handed him Mischief in his Christmas t-shirt, placing Maaca's son next to his mother in line on Santa's lap.

So far, things had been going smoothly, if I didn't count the look of contempt Maaca had accorded Santa's gift of a hat. I cautiously placed Bear into Santa's left hand. As I'd hoped, Bear allowed me to affix the hat to his head and tie the straps under his chin. Though he was as proud and regal as his grandmother, he fortunately stopped short of patterning his behavior after Queen Victoria. And for once, Mischief and Bear seemed to be behaving themselves, although I had rarely known the two to sit touching each other's sides without grumbling.

I quickly accepted another piece of Christmas apparel offered by Mrs. Claus, a bright red and green striped scarf. I put the scarf around the neck of Bear's son Ivory, the fourth generation, and handed him into Mrs. Claus' right hand. Grateful for the continuing calm, I placed the final dog, Ivory's little daughter Jingles into Mrs. Claus' left hand and stepped back.

Before my bulk could clear the view of the Christmas setting, Bear growled at Mischief, and Mischief reached over and snapped at Bear. So much for family harmony!

"Don't do that, son." Santa's voice was gentle and smooth as his gloved hand reached to reinforce his words by patting Mischief on the head.

At which point Mischief bit Santa's hand.

Smoothly but firmly, the gloved hand picked up the little red-and-white hellion, passed him to Mrs. Claus and

112

said, "Just put this little gentleman on the end, Dear. He's not getting anything in his stocking but coals this year."

The camera and lighting crew and helping elves [generally known as SPCA volunteers at other times of the year] cracked up. Amid soft laughter, Santa reshuffled the line-up of five small dogs and the cameras clicked. I quickly offered my apologies for my children-in-fur's behavior, thanked the Clauses and the helpers, and departed with my brood, little expecting to ever see my Christmas-picture Santa again.

The Christmas picture, when developed, showed an unruffled Santa and wife with four small dogs across their two laps who faced the camera nicely and a fifth one who sat on the end and refused to face the camera – or the music. I tried hard to get in the spirit of Christmas and to send copies of the little group's picture out with cards. Somehow I never found the time or the heart, but it wasn't for the lack of trying.

I'd closed us all into the TV room one night, so I didn't have to wonder which trashcan this or that one had overturned and what other destructive adventures they could instigate. I tried to concentrate on the upcoming holiday season and fun and to address some cards. Sunny and Rusty weren't especially happy with the arrangements because the closed door prevented their favorite game of chasing each other all through the house. Mostly I'd stared at the TV, my mind blank and my fingers still. Suddenly, I realized Sunny the cat was sitting on the top of the TV, reaching over to the door just beside the console and running his paw around the knob of the door. He was very intent on his task.

It took a while for my foggy thinking to realize that he was attempting to open the door. Never having had cats before, I'd never considered how they learn and grow. As I watched Sunny, I realized that he'd observed me opening the door by turning the knob and was trying to imitate my actions. And if he'd been blessed with an opposing segment to his paw that replicated a human thumb, he'd have had the door open.

The night's efforts produced no cards to mail to friends and family but it certainly heightened my appreciation of the thinking abilities of cats, at least the big yellow one who shared my life.

The only puppy or young dog who seems uninterested in playing with Sunny was little Laddie, who didn't appear interested in going to any other home either. With his bobbed tail, Laddie was not going to make it to the show ring despite a beautiful coat, movement and everything else, and I made many attempts to find him his own home where he could have a family to himself and not have to compete with the rest of the older pack. But each new family that came to meet him was greeted with cool rejection. After the fifth or sixth try, I gave up and decided he wanted to remain on the fringe but never joining in the activities of the Astra mob.

Fourteen months later, the freakish Williamsburg weather coughed up a snowstorm with five inches of snow followed by another inch of ice to keep the fluffy stuff in place. It was long past dark when I arrived home from work and from dropping off a prescription at Mother's apartment. I failed to notice that the gate of my fenced yard was standing open, the ice having counteracted the heavy iron ball on the chain designed to pull it closed.

By the time I shed work suit and heels, donned comfortable clothes, and called the dogs to come back inside, two puppies and three older dogs were missing. Six hours later, I'd managed to retrieve all but one, a seven-pound young female named Happy. In the icy stillness past midnight, I could only hope that she'd found a warm haven. This little papillon had never spent more than an hour outdoors at one time in her whole life, except at an outdoor

Paw Prints Through The Years

dog show when she was protected from sun or rain or the elements by woven mats and shade tarps. Now she was lost in a hostile environment where temperatures were in the single digits.

For the next three-and-a-half weeks, I posted flyers advertising a reward for my missing dog. I haunted dog pounds, humane societies, and ran ads in the newspaper. To no avail! The continuing frigid winter weather dimmed and finally killed my hopes of finding my Happy alive. Freezing temperatures protected the original layer of snow and ice, and two more snowstorms added another five inches to the blanket of dirty white, which had become a seemingly constant characteristic of my world.

I grieved. The optimist in me hoped that this gregarious little girl, who'd never met a human she didn't like or trust, had found a caring place with someone else. The pessimist in me   still searched for a small, black-and-white body.

Twenty-six days after Happy's disappearance, a deep male voice on the phone asked if I'd lost a little dog.

"Yes," I choked, trying not to shout.

"Well, my wife and I have been putting out feed and water for this little black-and-white dog that is loose in the woods across from the Cracker Barrel. She won't come to us, but she does eat the food we put out."

"When did you see her? Was she okay?" By this time, I was almost screaming with excitement. "How big is she?" I injected, before he could answer my first two questions, conscious that the dog he described might not be my Happy.

"Very small. She just came out of the woods about fifteen minutes ago and went up to the little dish of food we'd set out," replied the voice. "If you can drive over to the parking lot of the Cracker Barrel, I'll show you where she went back into the woods."

115

Jean C. Keating

I ran one stoplight, cut off two other cars, and arrived in only a bit less elapsed time than could have been achieved by teleporting. I found an elderly couple standing beside their car waiting for me.

Kindly eyes beneath white brows focused on my strained face as I threw open my car door. I noted without assimilating it that the couple's car tag said "CLAUS 2" and that the faces of the waiting couple looked familiar. The woman smiled and waved to me before getting back into their car to escape the icy wind. The white-haired and white-bearded man came to meet me.

"You're Jean." It was a statement rather than a question. Directing my gaze across the street, the gentle voice continued, "See that little blue bowl over there on the ground?"

"Yes." I nodded agreement.

"That's a dish of food we put out about thirty minutes ago. She's already been out and eaten some of the food, but each time we try to get any closer she goes back into the break between the trees there and disappears. Perhaps if you were to over and call her ..." he began.

I was half way across the street before he could finish his sentence, but he wasn't far behind me. I walked into the woods about three steps, and began to call, "Here, Happy. DinDin."

A flash of black-and-white popped up out of the ground. She flung herself in the direction of my face, jumping upward with the spring that is so characteristic of paps. After more than three weeks of cold and loneliness, she leaped aloft in front of me, still confident that I would reach out and catch her in mid-air. I hugged her tightly and buried my face in her snow-drenched coat to cover the tears that I could not stop.

"I offered a reward, but I never heard a word until now." It was difficult to talk coherently with the precious wiggling body in my arms raining doggie kisses on my face. "You don't know how grateful I am that you called, or how much I appreciate what you and your wife have done in feeding and caring for her." I was shaking with joy that my little Happy was alive and capable of jumping.

The man reached to pat the dainty head of the dog in my arms. I realized that his hand shivered a little, and that my own face was icy from the cold wind and wet kisses.

"Let's get her back in my car, and I'll give you a check for the reward," I said.

"Oh, my wife and I won't take any reward," he responded, as we turned and re-crossed the road to our respective cars. "We have two dogs of our own and would hope that anyone who found them would help as we've tried to do."

With the twinkle in his eye of an adoring parent, he added, "Would you like to see their pictures?"

"Of course," I nodded and reached for the picture he'd pulled from his billfold. Against a background of a magnificent Christmas tree, Mr. and Mrs. Santa Claus, my Christmas-picture Santa and his wife, sat and held two fluffy shih tzus. The same background, the same couple who'd just reunited my darling Happy and me. Suddenly my brain put the pieces together. I realized what the car tag meant and why the couple had looked so familiar.

"Oh," I stammered. "You and your wife! You're the ones who helped me with a Christmas picture of five generations of my papillons. I can't believe this. How wonderful to meet you again."

"And how is the little rascal that bit my thumb?" Santa chuckled. No hesitation. He'd know from the start just where he'd met me before.

"Feisty as ever," I replied, trying to hold on to the small body of the little rascal's daughter I held in my arms, while covering the fact that it had taken me this long to recognize the couple. "Can't I at least take you and your wife to dinner or something?"

"No," he responded firmly with a final pat on Happy's head. "Donate what you wish to the humane society."

He collected his picture of his own precious shih tzus, waved goodbye and drove away.

Later that afternoon, my vet's exam could find little wrong with my precious Happy. She'd lost two of her seven pounds, but was not dehydrated nor did she show any signs of hypothermia on paws or ear tips. Except for the weight loss and a reluctance to go outside for some weeks she showed no sign of wear.

The vet visit was my second stop of the afternoon after getting my Happy dog back. My first stop was the humane society where I gave them a check for the promised reward. I didn't want to get in bad with Santa. I knew he'd be watching. I didn't want coals in *my* stockings.

Living With Dementia

With Happy's safe return, it was a little easier to deal with the stress of being caretaker to an increasingly angry and frightened mother. I learned far more by accident about dementia than from all my reading and research. One evening I called Mother from work at 4:45, telling her to be ready and meet me in the lobby of her retirement complex at 6:00 pm when I got home from Richmond. I carefully explained that I needed to quickly pick her up and get her to a dentist appointment at 6:20 pm, since the dentist was staying late as a special favor to her and to me.

She went down to the lobby immediately, grew madder and madder as I didn't come. When she ranted to the attendant at the receptions desk that I was always late, was supposed to meet her at 6:00 pm and such, the attendant tried to tell her that it was only a little after 5:00 pm and that she was too early, had gotten the time confused and was an hour early. Mother just got angry and tried to hit the attendant with her cane, saying the receptionist was telling her she couldn't tell time. I was always keeping her waiting.

Jean C. Keating

By the time I got over to pick her up, at 5:55 pm, Mother was so mad she fussed and threatened all the way to the dental appointment. I really never knew whether the concept of time was distorted or whether the fear and stress of a dental appointment had pushed her into such a state.

Like many other nights, it was a relief to get home to my little four-legged family members who always welcomed me with cute tricks, wagging tails and happy faces. After the frustrations of trying to analyze and deal with Mother's unpredictability, it was refreshing to watch the interactions of the pack with each other and with me and to try to figure out how they were thinking about life.

Most of the time, their constant warmth and affection went a long way toward relieving the stress of my days. At other times, their chicanery made me wonder if I had any brains. Since I had more little people to tend and less time to devote to them, I got the stupid idea that a doggie door would be a wonderful addition to save time letting little ones in and out. It was only after investing time, effort and money into getting one installed that I realized they used it to avoid having to stay outside and potty. It wasn't that they didn't immediately figure out how it worked. It was that they never wanted to stay outside, would not use it to go out, and would only use it to come back into the house. I'd turn them out the side door in the mornings and evenings and they would run around and come in the doggie door into the sunroom and potty. Great dog trainer that I am, I solved the problem by leaving the lock on the doggie door, rendering it useless.

My attempted solutions to problems with my mother were about as effective. She complained that I never got home in time to help her with getting to the doctor or to her hairdresser. Since the doctor came to the retirement complex and his office was between the dining room where she ate every day and the small beauty shop where she had her hair done weekly, it was hard for me to understand why she couldn't walk five more steps and take herself to these things. But I had learned not to attempt logic with her and hired an eldercare nurse to take her to these things during the day while I was at work. It worked about as well as the doggie door idea. My mother wanted my attention. Having another's help didn't suit her interests at all, so she picked fights with the nurse, threatening to hit her, and in general made life difficult for everyone she could.

Fortunately, Mischief proved to be a better analytical thinker than I the night his dam developed breathing problems. Maaca had suffered with congestive heart failure for almost three years and was on medications to strengthen the heartbeat and on diuretics to control the buildup of fluids around her lungs. As usual, we'd gone out for one last potty break, gone upstairs to bed and I'd crashed. Thunderstorms don't usually awaken me during the first two hours of sleep. The roof falling in might, but it took a lot to drag me back to consciousness in those early hours of sleep. But Mischief managed by standing on my chest, pawing the covers off me, and digging at my neck and face until he got me awake and focused. He backed away only when I sat up and turned to help his dam. He'd first have to reason that his dam needed help, that he needed his human, and then to figure out how to awaken me. He'd succeeded admirably with all three points. Regrettably, her vet and I were not so successful, although we struggled until nearly dawn to save her.

The look she gave me a little after four in the morning said without the need of words, "I'm tired of trying. Please let me go."

I whispered, "It's all right. You can let go. We'll make it without you somehow. But wait for me at Rainbow Bridge." She collapsed in my arms as I added, "Vaya con Dios", and she was gone.

I was not nearly over the loss of Maaca when my life

Jean C. Keating

was diminished again by the lost of my friend, confidant, and much beloved ex-mother-in-law who died in her sleep at 91. The bizarre series of phone messages from my own mother during the weekend I was away in New York for Mom's funeral convinced me, as nothing else had, that it was time to move my mother to a nursing home.

I'd sent Mother's nurse over to take her grocery shopping at 10:00 am on Saturday. The nurse's notes showed that she reminded Mother verbally and in writing that I was away in New York at a funeral. Between noon on Saturday and my return on Monday afternoon, my mother logged a series of 79 voice mail messages, many of them coming at ten and fifteen minute intervals during the day and late into the evening. Breaks corresponding to dinner hours showed she did stop to eat. The tragic characteristic of the messages was their descent into anger and fear that this elderly woman generated from her own conversations with a recorded message that said, "I can't come to the phone right now. Leave your number and I'll call you back"

Message number one was a bright, cutesy twitter that said, "There's a craft show downstairs. Come over and go with me."

By message number five, the voice sounded hurt and said, "If you're mad at me, please come over and tell me what's wrong."

By message number ten, the voice was whining and saying, "Do you want to get rid of me? Do you want me to go back to Georgia?"

Shortly thereafter, because these messages were being logged about eight minutes apart now, the voice was quavering as it said, "You'll have to help me get back to Georgia. I don't know how to go, but since you want me to, I'll go."

By message number forty, it was late evening on Saturday and the voice revealed anger as it threatened,

Paw Prints Through The Years

"You can't make me go back to Georgia. I'm going to tell people you steal my social security money."

I didn't want to see the hopelessness of the problem. I wanted to believe I could fix it. I tried bringing in a psychologist. Mother wouldn't see him at first, and then was defensive and uncooperative when she did talk with him. He pronounced that she resented the loss of control that a health-care nurse had imposed and prescribed that fewer things be done for her by the nurse, directing that she get herself to the doctor's appointments and to her hair appointments. She called Social Services and reported that she was being starved; only allowed one meal a day to eat, and being abused. They investigated and recommended a nursing home. I wanted to hold out for assisted living arrangements, something, anything, but the surrender of all freedoms that a nursing home brings. But professionals in the geriatric field warned me that little changes just wouldn't work, that like the thermostat and the voice mail, little changes would not be understood. Moving her every year or ever two years as she worsened was not realistic because of the long time to acclimate to a new situation. The sad truth about this hateful disease is that little changes are enormously stressful, confusing and threatening – so sadly, I bowed to necessity and downsized her apartment to a simple room in a skilled care facility.

Meanwhile, back at the Astra digs, Holy had decided that I wasn't pushing Minerva at him, so maybe he'd take a second look. I came home from dealing with a very angry mother who did not want to be in a nursing home and was intent on calling me every dirty name she could remember, including the 'B' word she objected to my using with my dogs, to find three adorable little girls had been added to my life. Astra's Opulent Ounce, called Dixie, would grow up to become the foundation bitch of the Keepsake papillons. Astra's Ohme Ohmy, called Little, would develop the gorgeous ears of her granddam Fallon. She'd inherited the solid head of her sire, though in a deep mahogany red, so she was never shown. But she would produce some beautiful puppies that would shine in the show ring. Astra's Onyx Original, called Nikki, would become my therapy over the next few years, as we returned together to the world of dog shows.

One other astonishing thing happened during these frustrating days of dealing with my mother's failing mind. A father and daughter came to visit on Saturday just to see some papillons. I told them I had nothing for adoption, having long ago accepted that Laddie didn't want to leave the Astra pack. During their visit, almost the entire Astra pack, augmented by Sunny, were jumping on and off the sofa where the two visitors sat talking about papillons. I always like to test the patience and tolerance of prospective human companions. Suddenly Laddie came into the living room, an unusual event in itself by a little boy who usually avoided being seen by visitors. He took one sniff or look or whatever of the young high school student on the sofa and pushed his way to take center stage in her lap.

I tried to continue on with my conversation, but my mind was reeling from shock. The father was explaining that he'd promised to get his daughter a papillon for her high school graduation present and they were pleased to get to meet some. Laddie was a young adult, not a puppy. Not what these two were seeking. I was agonizing on how to explain to them that Laddie had picked her to be his own, that he'd refused all other families. I feared his little heart was destined for disappointment, that they would reject his overtures just as he had rejected so many families who wanted him. I should have given the strong-willed little fellow more credit from the beginning. Suddenly the young woman asked, "How about this little one? Would he be available for adoption?"

Paw Prints Through The Years

It seemed the attraction between them was strong and true, that both human and papillon felt the pull. Laddie went home with them and never looked back. Just how he had known to wait for that one person, that one perfect home I will never know. But he had. In the years to come, I would visit them or talk to them about their lives together. All the Shealy family members dotted on him, fixing him rockfish [his favorite] and eggs for Saturday breakfasts, taking him for rides on their boat, and pampering him as all papillons deserve. But everyone else was forgotten when his Kristin was around. I sometimes wonder how she is going to explain to any prospective husband-to-be that Laddie intends to accompany them on the honeymoon.

Dear Friends and Family,

Mama Jean never seems to catch up on things anymore. So as the senior member of the pack, I'm going to write a Christmas letter and try to bring

you all up to date with the Astra gang. Maybe left with only the addressing, Mama Jean can manage to get the mail out before Christmas ...

maybe! I sure hope Fallon and I don't have to do envelopes, because I always get those sticky label things attached to the bottoms of my paws, and I don't like it at all. It just isn't dignified for the leader of the pack.

I know that some of you have considered the possibility that we'd all fallen off the edge of the earth. Well, we fell into what Mama Jean described as a very deep hole, but are trying to crawl out at last. Granny Kitty has taken a lot of attention over the last few years, and we'd about given up on celebrating and communicating and all that stuff. But things seem a bit freer now, and there even seems to be this little green tree with all sorts of toys hanging off it that is sitting on a table in the living room. Mama Jean gets grumpy when we try to remove the little toys that are on it. I wish someone would tell me why. They're a lot more interesting than most of the pretty colored packages under the tree, even if some of those packages do smell like they might be for me!

Since I have the computer controls, I'll start with news about ME. I'm doing well, despite the fact that my archrival, Sunny the cat, pushed me off the upstairs hallway into the entrance way some six weeks ago. Despite my advanced age – I'll bet you've all forgotten that I'll be fifteen next month – I came through it with bruises to both body and dignity, but not a bit of change in my attitude about charging at that awful cat!

Misty, the other cat, is much easier to have around. She mostly stays to herself or on Mama Jean's desk and doesn't try to get in my way. My dam Maaca and dear old Peanut have gone to play at Rainbow Bridge where the weather is always warm and their tired old bodies are refreshed and no longer a bother to them. Sable just went to sleep one night and decided to join them.

My son Bear is still a pain. He seems to think he should be running the pack, but at least he doesn't invade the second floor and I can have some peace as the senior bed dog. Fallon is as sweet and lovely as ever. Our three granddaughters worry us a lot less with their noise since both she and I have gone a little deaf. Well, make that a lot deaf! Anyway, the girls have won lots of ribbons and points this year, but none have managed to get it totally correct and bring home a CHAMPION title for themselves. Oh, well! There's always next year!

Granny Kitty is doing well. In March she had cataract surgery on one eye and is now reading great. She moved to a senior care facility from her apartment in the retirement village. The move was a bumpy ride for her and for Mama Jean, but the pack and I have been very consoling and comforting. Fallon and I really love Granny's new place because we get to go into more of the rooms and visit the people and they all like to hold us and give us treats. Sometimes Bear and Holy come along, and the four of us really create a lively stir in the place.

Feisty Granny Kitty had a bit of a problem settling in. She got into a fistfight with one of the other residents and hit one of the aids with her cane on another occasion, but things appear to have settled now. She's gained a little weight and has decided she likes Bingo. I tried to help by tasting these little blue markers she plays with, but she didn't seem to appreciate my efforts. Best of all, the nurses there make certain Granny takes her medications and Mama Jean isn't always running off to try to deal with that problem. So Jean has more time for playing with me and the Astra gang.

Auntie Barb isn't needed for eldercare nursing for Granny any more, so Mama Jean has arranged for her to become our nanny. She comes over to play with us every day. Now when Jean rushes off to work every morning, we have someone to let us out and play with us and brush us. Most of it is a great improvement. We seem to get a lot more baths, however, and I could do without those!

I do believe, yes, I see I'm right! Jean has finally put those nasty stickers on some envelopes for me. So on behalf of the Astra gang, you and yours are wished the merriest of holidays and a healthy, happy new year. I think I'll go check out that little stuffed rabbit I just saw Sunny take off the tree.

Mischief

Astra's Mischief Maaca

Hello Again

The responses from many friends to the Christmas letter were warm and supportive. I got lots of New Year cards and letters telling me how much friends understood my not finding time to write in so long, having dealt with or still being forced to deal with much the same caretakers' issues themselves. Hearing from friends was a wonderful start to the new year. Their sympathies and kindnesses made me sad and angry at the same time: sad that I'd not found time to stay in contact for many years and angry and distressed at the amount of lost time in others' lives as well as my own that was represented by the struggles with Alzheimer's.

The disease had some useful aspects however. An ice storm prevented my getting to the nursing home to celebrate Christmas with Mother, so we moved the celebration to the next day when the roads were finally clear enough to allow me to get my car out. It mattered not at all to Mother, who happily showed off her new presents, especially the matching wooden canes I'd given her and her best buddy. I'd hoped they could distinguish between their canes, but neither they nor I could remember which one had the fox headed cane and which one the bird headed cane. So they spent much of their time discussing whether or not they had the right cane. At least both canes were rubber tipped to prevent slipping and not nearly as heavy as the metal one when she started swinging it instead of using it for balance.

I'd finally found a present that I thought I really wanted. The 500-piece interlocking puzzle included a brief mystery story for which the face of the finished puzzle provided the final clue. After putting the puzzle together by candlelight, since the ice storm knocked out power for a few days, it was too dim to see the details of the puzzle well enough to solve the mystery. At least that was my excuse. It had nothing to do with the difficulty of completing the puzzle while cats walked across the pieces, scattering them on the floor and requiring them to be retrieved from bored doggies' mouths.

Bear developed a persistent skin problem. Small black encrusted circles would appear on his skin. These spots most resembled dirt, but when washed turned red, spread slightly and resulted in hair loss within the site. Skin tests and blood work showed no reason for the problem. I changed shampoos, food, supplements, detergents used on his bedding, cleaning solutions used on his crate and surrounding areas. Nothing helped. Although he remained a steady and happy eater, he never gained above his trim five plus pounds and would, from time to time, drop an eighth of an ounce for no reason. Nothing slowed his enthusiasm or his constant struggles for status and space, however. On Christmas day he'd gotten past me and managed to mate with Minerva before I could run across the yard to prevent it. So shortly before the first of March, we had new little people, two tiny boys I named Toy Tank and Time Traveler.

Shortly after the boys' birth, I noticed that Sunny the cat had developed a new talent. He'd taken up puppy-sitting. About three weeks after the birth of puppies, Mother Nature begins to take a hand in their weaning by supplying puppies with very sharp little needles in their previously soft mouths. Mother dogs respond by suddenly finding more and more activities away from the whelping and nursing area. Unfortunately, puppies still have little temperature control at this age, so they will cry even when a heat lamp and water bottle are furnished to make up for their dam's absence. I was aware that Sunny watched Minerva closely from the vantage point of the dining room table as she went about her motherly duties, but accepted him as just another funny and large sized dog.

One day when Minerva went out for a little rest and relaxation and left the two tiny boys alone in the sleeping box, I turned on the lamp, put in the hot water bottle, covered them with a receiving blanket and went about my business. When I glanced in a bit later, all I could see in the sleeping box was a very large, golden tabby stretched out with a smug look on his face. Between choking and trying to start my heart up again, I reached for Sunny. I thought he'd eaten the puppies. I was mentally kicking myself for being careless, cursing him for being a cat.

My grab for the cat was arrested by the appearance from beneath his upper back leg of two tiny front paws and a puppy's head. With heart still skipping beats and doing flips, I lifted the cat's top hind leg to find both little boys snugly lying on Sunny's inner thigh, enjoying the warmth of the big cat's body and long furry tail to keep them comfortable during their mother's absence. The silly grin on Sunny's face announced his satisfaction with his self-appointed role.

As the puppies grew, Sunny spent more and more time in the pen with the boys and Minerva spent more and more time out and about. I began to watch Sunny for a cue as to when Minerva wanted to go outside. He'd climb on the table and make eye contact with the dog to check on when she needed his puppy sitting services; she'd amble over to the side of the pen and stretch. I'd let her out and Sunny would replace her in the pen. I forgot about the heat lamp and the water bottle. The big lug never missed an opportunity to sit with his boys.

When the time came for them to come out of their playpen and stumble around on the floor, Sunny was right there to play with them. I put little leads on them, left the leash portion dangling and Sunny made of game of leash training them. So I guess maybe it wasn't such a crazy idea after all to bring two little kittens home to join the Astra pack.

Mischief turned fifteen on the ninth of January. We planned a small party to celebrate and invited his friends from Gloucester to join us for doggie and human treats. One of his friends was a big, black lab named Dumbo. He came and accepted some treats but seemed very uncomfortable with the mob of smaller dogs running everywhere and retreated to the safety of his owner's vehicle with his present, a giant chew bone. Mischief exchanged presents with his little pals, but came out way ahead. One of them gave him a big, raw steak and he enjoyed small portions of 'his steak' nightly for about a week after his birthday. He watched them open their presents of toys and tiny treats, more or less resigned to letting the other dogs keep them, all the while wearing his tiny birthday hat perched on his head. When the people food was served, however, he jumped up on the dining room chair and demanded his share. After all, it was his birthday!

One of my treasured photos of that day was a picture of my tiny boy, birthday hat half off the side of his head, sitting in a dining room chair acting his part as King of the House.

The future looked a lot brighter for me. Demands on my time as caretaker were sharply diminished with Mother in the nursing facility. I had more time to spend with my little people in fur and to enjoy my career. But extra time brought the opportunity for more reflective thinking. Once it was possible to get past putting out brush fires and dealing with crisis management, I had time to reflect on peripheral events and stop and consider what the gathering clouds of political machinations might mean in my future, five years down the line.

After nearly twenty years, my agency head had been forced out by political maneuvering. Replacing knowledgeable board members with young people who helped acquire campaign contributions by stuffing envelopes may be politically expedient. Such individuals, in my opinion, had no place in deciding the worth of doctoral program proposals. As political connections rather than professional knowledge drove more and more appointments, many of the staff with which I'd worked, respected and trusted during two decades began to leave in protest. While data and research are needed irrespective of political party, I knew that I would never be happy in an environment that I feared would more and more entail pressures to slant the statistics rather than acknowledge the existence of problems. I began to contemplate what I should do, and finally decided that I didn't have to do anything.

Dogs and cats, unlike two-legged children and family, don't need money for college, and need far smaller trust funds because of their much shorter life expectancy. By my birthday, I'd decided that my gift to the Astra gang and to me was to retire early and spend more time at home in my garden with my fur family. As it turned out, it would be very boring and would lead eventually to a third career, but that would come later.

The Grass is Always Greener

Sweltering humidity and high 80's temperature at 7:45 in the morning didn't improve my grumpy disposition. Neither did the happy noises from the parking lot some 400 feet behind my back fence. Excited voices reverberated off the trees that blocked my view of the College of William and Mary Hall's parking lot. My canine pack barked excitedly at the intermittent rise in noise level, then looked at me to be certain I was not going to growl at them to be quiet.

The Antiques Road Show had arrived in my own backyard. Not satisfied with bumping some of my favorite shows off the HGTV channel, this newest craze in Americana had now invaded my home, leastwise the noise had now invaded my yard! And I couldn't change the channel and drown the human hordes out either! For the next two days I would, I knew, be treated to loudly talking people traversing the parking lot behind the stand of trees in my back yard. Hordes of humans would emerge from vehicles of all sizes carrying or dragging all sorts of goofy things to the large convention center in the distance.

I grumbled as I dragged around the yard, spilling

coffee from the cup I held in my left hand while I tried to dead-head the previous day's blooms from twenty-five or more different varieties of day lilies. I totally ignored the beauty of the blooms which brightened the yard in a showy display and the leaf shapes and shades of green from numerous hostas that provided a background to the colorful day lilies.

Retirement had not been the blessing I'd envisioned. After I'd slept late and napped every day for a week, I needed something else to do. I missed the sense of accomplishment I'd derived from my career. Leisure time was nice, in that I'd now had the luxury of time to get to some long postponed projects. I'd painted the dogs' room, had new flooring put down in the dogs' room and the laundry room, had the car painted, and won a few battles in the never-ending war with weeds in my flower beds. The dogs had been to a few shows, and even won some points, but those were their accomplishments more than mine.

I missed the staff I'd worked with over two decades. I'd hired them all, worked with them in respectful harmony and mutual trust for years, and counted them not just as colleagues but as friends. When I'd announced to them that I would retire in June, they'd broken a long-agreed-upon rule not to celebrate birthdays by throwing me a surprise party with food and presents and decorations. I walked through the sultry heat of early morning in my garden holding a coffee cup that had been one of those presents, one proclaiming "If Older Is Better, I Must Be Approaching Magnificent!" The cup accentuated my sense of loss.

I missed the colleagues from the eighty-seven institutions of higher education with whom I'd worked. They'd surprised me with a special tribute at the luncheon of their spring meeting with presents and a framed resolution commending and commemorating our mutual achievements and ending with a phrase that brought tears to my eyes at the recognition of how well they knew me: "We request of her, in her retirement, to remember us with the same kindness, loyalty, and sufferance which she has always held for small canine creatures." The beautiful framed resolution graced a central spot in my living room. Their gift, a butterfly garden statue rendered in copper with colored marbles forming the body of the butterfly, winked at me in the early morning sunlight. It reminded me of just how much I missed the shared challenges and achievements with this wonderful group.

My co-workers, my colleagues from the institutions, and many other friends had honored me with a grand retirement luncheon. Turning the numerous photographs and memorabilia into memory book pages and sending thank-you notes to them all had kept me linked to that part of my life for awhile. But now it was done and over, and I felt diminished, left behind, finished. I engaged in one of the worst self-pity parties since my divorce almost two decades before, and the happy invitations from my canine pack to play with them were ignored. I looked backward and saw my life as over.

Morning coffee enriched with fat-free Cool Whip gradually mellowed my disposition and turned my mind to wondering what it would be like to join the happy throngs of Antique Road Showers who continued to disrupt my quiet existence with their noise. What is the expression about not criticizing a fellow until you've walked a mile in his moccasins?

The dogs relaxed as the tenseness of my body language eased. They ran with wild abandon around the garden. Even a baby squirrel came out to chirp noisily at the dogs beneath the willow oak to which his nest was questionably attached. But the squirrel reminded me of the sadness of losing Bear, who'd died just shortly before I retired. Bear's greatest playmate was a wild squirrel that teased him by waiting on the deck rail for Bear to come outside before charging madly just a few feet ahead of the little papillon. Squirrel would race across the yard and up a tree inches before Bear could reach him. It was probably one of this little fellow's parents. Now that Bear was gone, the older squirrel ceased his teasing. None of the other papillons in the family were acceptable substitutes it seemed. And this baby didn't indicate that he intended to take up that particular game.

I was still grieving over Bear's loss. We'd struggled with his skin problem for more than two years, but I had not realized there was anything seriously wrong with him until I found the lymph glands in his throat and groin swollen. Biopsies showed a vicious, quickly moving cancer. He was gone in less than five weeks. He'd never managed to take over the pack; his father Mischief was still alive and in charge. I consoled myself with the fact that his last few weeks were spent as a bed dog, with Mischief's grumbling acceptance if not enthusiastic consent. And he'd gone with me to work almost every day of his final two weeks, to be coddled and cared for as best I could. My head knew that all that could have been done had been. My heart still hurt.

I tried to redirect my melancholy thoughts to something other than the absence of Bear's joyful presence in my morning garden. I began to fantasize about what I might take to the Antiques Roads Show. The grouch that lived in my mind with me, said "Oh, right! This makes sense! You can't stand the noise, so now you're going to join them!"

Fantasy warred with realism. I considered an old chest that belonged to my great-grandfather. It was upstairs and something I thought would be fun to have appraised. Then I remembered that it had taken three grown men to get it up the stairs to my second floor. I wasn't likely to drag that down and across to the show by myself. So I abandoned that idea as too much trouble.

Paw Prints Through The Years

Then I considered smaller things, like the comic books I still had from childhood and the ones I'd bought in the 1970's when I reentered a phase of collecting. A deeper consideration of that possibility caused me to abandon that idea also. I knew very well the worth of many of the comics, and was not interested in having any so-called expert get his grubby hands – and hand oil – all over them. Nor was I likely to haul them out of air-conditioned vaults to expose to the heat and humidity of that sultry, summer morning.

I probed my memory for something small and portable that I might consider taking across the way to the Antique Road Show. I remembered one small bit of memorabilia that wasn't addressed by comic catalogue and one I'd never considered evaluating. I had an autographed picture of Roy Rogers from about 1942. Even as I wondered why that particular item came to mind, I remembered the reason. Sadly I'd just moved it to my memory book along with newspaper clippings of his death. Another of my childhood heroes lost.

Mischief took advantage of the temporary cessation of my walking to take a short nap at my feet, his tongue hanging limply out the side of his mouth and panting in the rising temperature. Two young dogs ran exuberantly through the flowerbeds, colliding with each other and falling against an ancient marker made by my mother's father's father's father. I reached to straighten it and realized that in it I had a real, honest-to-goodness antique and one that was movable, well, sort of movable anyway. Thanks to the whack already afforded the ancient piece by my two fur-children, the marker came up easily from the dirt moistened by the previous night's rain. Georgia marble isn't light, but it is durable.

My however-many-greats grandfather was a farmer, not a stonemason. His work was a labor of love if not a lovely labor. Most of the lines were worn beyond recognition.

Jean C. Keating

But the sentiment of the verse came through across the years: "Yesterdays are over and unchangeable, tomorrows may never come, all we have is today." It was still a heavy piece, if not as readable as when my distant ancestor carved it and gave it to his young wife so many generations ago.

It would afford a story to the appraiser; it was old and had been handed down in the family since the turn of the nineteenth century. Between patting heads that pushed from one side or the other for attention before returning to romping through the flower beds, I pondered my response to the second question always asked by experts on this show, "Do you have any idea of the value of this piece?"

I considered the question as I looked around me with clearer sight. Daylilies painted the yard in reds, oranges, pinks, yellows and all combinations in between. Each bloom had only one day of life, opening almost visibly as one watched. The blooms didn't waste time fretting that the one day of life was overcast, rainy, sunny, or too blasted hot. They bloomed forth bringing beauty to those who would see, and bounty to visiting bees. By evening, they would close their petals and by tomorrow those petals would dry and fall to the ground to enrich the soil, while other buds would take up the work of drenching the yard in rainbow hues.

The dogs made happy yipping sounds as they ran and frolicked in the yard, unmindful of the climbing temperatures and oppressive humidity. The tiny squirrel joined their play from above with mock challenges, enjoying his status as junior member of his clan. He was undaunted by the chore of growing up quickly and helping with storing nuts and supplies before winter.

I brushed some remaining black dirt from the base of the garden marker. It was just an old piece of marble, badly carved with an old truism. But it reminded me that life was what you made it. Making the most of each day we have was a lesson we can learn from the flowers and from the animals that bless our gardens. It was a lesson carved in marble that reached across the generations to serve as a much needed attitude adjustment that morning.

My decision about joining the Antiques Road Show made, I returned the carved block of marble to the garden floor. I didn't need the 'expert' in my back yard to tell me its worth.

The late fall twilight held a hint of frost. It was hard to believe that nearly five months had passed since I'd taken up the challenge of writing a book. It had brought the sense of accomplishment I'd found wanting in my life. I was drained but contented as I relaxed with most of my little fur family happily playing about me in the yard. The white coats of the Astra gang were beginning to thicken with the approach of winter. They flickered silvery in the lights from the College's property that flooded through trees barren of leaves. I sat on the steps of the deck and watched their play. The two cats were somewhere in the house, curled contentedly in the relative warmth of the indoors.

Mischief curled against my leg, grumbling softly whenever any of the young males ran over to be petted. Fallon sat quietly leaning against my other leg. The two senior members of the pack ignored the yips and barks of the younger ones as they contested a stick one had found, trying to drag the three foot length of wood in four different directions at once. Toy Tank had gone to live in Richmond some two weeks before, but his brother Traveler had snookered Nikki and Little into playing the rough and tumbling games he'd enjoyed with his littermate.

Unable to get the hold he wanted on the stick, Traveler reached for the nearest handy object and grabbed the fringe on Nikki's ear. I reminded myself that she'd gotten her championship in the fall and didn't have to be so particular

Jean C. Keating

about that beautiful fringe, but force of habit almost brought a verbal correction from me. Nikki took care of the situation on her own, however, by letting go of the stick and nipping Traveler sharply on his foot.

Imp galloped over to take up a position in front of me and yipped sharply. The force of his effort to vocalize lifted his dainty front paws slightly off the grass. When I didn't respond, he repeated his original single yip in the same tone. I apologized as usual to one I affectionately called 'Johnnie One-Note' for not understanding what he was trying so hard to tell me.

Mischief's low grumbling sounded tired, as he should have been. We'd spent most of the day traveling and attending a critique group meeting that was some eighty minutes away by car. Mischief accompanied me everywhere now, except for trips to the grocery store or outings with friends which involved eating in restaurants. Some three months before, he'd started in with seizures. To keep him stable and to minimize the amount of medication needed, he got his little bits of prednisone crushed and mixed with Nutri-Cal three times a day. The critique group had gone into overtime that afternoon, and I'd pulled Mischief's medication out of his traveling pack, crushing and mixing his dosage almost on automatic, as I discussed options for improvements in one or another member's story. Mischief's response to taking his dosage of prednisone brought a chuckle from the group. My communication with Mischief seemed to be at a much higher level of understanding than with my other dogs. I only had to whisper softly, "Medicine" to gain his cooperation. He'd watched attentively as I mixed his medication with a fat lump of sticky and sweet nutrient, then rolled it on to the ball of my finger and offered it to him. He'd curl his lips away, hold his mouth open and wait patiently for me to smear the mixture on the roof of his mouth. The routine had brought laughter to the group this afternoon, which had pleased and excited my

142

little oldie so much that he'd stayed awake and alert during the entire drive home. Now he was having trouble keeping his eyes open.

One by one the rest of the pack tired of their outdoor play and came to stand on the deck with me or flopped on the rough wooden boards behind me. Finally only Traveler continued with his play. The long stick still fascinated him, even though he no longer had another dog pulling it away from him. He dropped it at my call and I rose and brought the pack inside to the warmer and brighter interior. They scattered to find toys from their toy box or favorite beds to sprawl in or to chase each other around the dining room table.

Mischief and Fallon claimed their favorite dog beds under my desk chair in the sunroom and I took advantage of an hour of free time between play and doggie dinners to mark up a segment of my dog mystery. Colleagues in the critique group had suggested a cleaner way with a segment of dialogue early in the day and I wanted to work on that section of my book while the comments were still fresh in my mind.

I'd made the decision to get on with something interesting and challenging in my life. And I'd written a mystery that featured a papillon. Naturally that literary character looked and acted like the favorite oldie that was curled at my feet during most of the writing, grumbling softly at any intrusion by younger pack members on his self-proclaimed private space.

December, 1998

Dear Friends and Family,

Last year you were all so appreciative of my poor efforts at communication that I thought I'd try again, if Sunny the cat will leave me alone. He

 wants to get in on the act, saying I'm feeble and need help. Not true, not true. All feline falsehoods! He just wants to get to MY keyboard.

So blame all the typos on him – his big paws don't fit on the keys.

Mama Jean retired in June. Our dear Auntie Barb still comes to play with us and we have Mama Jean home with us all the time too. It's great, but let me tell you, it is also very tiring on us geriatric companions. The first few weeks weren't so difficult, because Jean had tons of photographs of a glorious retirement luncheon to sort through and put into a memory book. So we had little to do but keep her company in the computer room.

Then she decided to redo the back room and the laundry room and paint the car and dozens of other projects, which kept us pacing the house and town. I tell you, my old body was worn out with keeping the *bad things* away while Mama Jean rumbled around doing this and that. Thank goodness we can keep her busy with addressing Christmas cards now, so Fallon and I can get a little breather from projects and just lie around in the computer room being the strong, silent companions we are.

We lost my son Bear this past May to a fast moving cancer. He left behind two new sons, born on February 25. Nikki finished her Championship in May, but she's not a bit stuck up about it. She plays with the rest of the pack as an equal, and we are all enjoying a great deal of yard time with this beautiful warm fall weather. Unfortunately, it seems never to rain anymore, so the gang and I have managed to turn the yard into a replica of the moon's surface with lots of mounds and craters.

I celebrated my fifteenth birthday with a lovely party back in January. In a few weeks, I'll be doing it again to mark my sixteenth. That's getting up toward 90 in human terms, which is about what

Granny Kitty is now. But I'm a lot more agile that Granny as I point out to her each time I go to visit.

Granny is doing very well, enjoying movies, bingo and weekly sing-a-longs. I thought the singing was terrible and don't intend to be visiting any more while that's going on, but the group over at the nursing home seemed to enjoy it a lot. Granny was invited to ride in the Center's van in the Christmas parade and she's still basking in the glow. If she shows me the photo one more time, I'm going to chew it up though. She didn't invite me to join her, and I don't think that was nice.

Mama Jean joined a writers' group last month and has gotten very excited with the feedback from members on her novel. She'd been ready to send it off to some publishers, but now plans to make a few changes and try to market it herself. I'm really, really tired of hearing her read it to me and Fallon, so I'm delighted she now has human friends willing to listen. Especially since these friends welcome me at the meetings. I'm deaf so I can just ignore all the humans reading this and that to each other and just look handsome sleeping on a pillow.

Sunny insists on getting his story into this letter. I will not tell them that I'm bossy, you big yellow dog you. Time to go! Have a great holiday and a wonderful new year.

Mischief

Astra's Mischief Maaca

Be Careful What You Pray For

We got so busy with writing the book that we completely forgot about planning a party for Mischief's sixteenth birthday. I think he was just as happy, because Fallon, he and I went out to a fast food chicken place and he had his own broiled chicken piece and a long ride in the car. I'm sure he told all the other dogs about it when we got home, because none of them would eat their regular dinner in protest.

The mystery book had kept me focused and challenged. Mysteries and science fiction novels were my two favorite types of relaxation, but I'd always been very critical of plots and clues in mysteries. In the early weeks of this last year of the century I rued the day I'd thrown a book across the floor with a derogatory comment of, "I could write one a lot better than that." In my defense, the book I'd thrown in disgust had named as murderer someone who walked into one scene on page 54 but was never mentioned before or after until the final three pages. It offended my sense of fair play.

Not too surprisingly, I discovered that criticizing was much easier than actually writing a mystery in the first place.

Paw Prints Through The Years

I've never found anyone who could beat Agatha Christie for plots and clues. My goal, since I needed a mountain to climb, a reason to face forward and not pine for the past, was to write a mystery with as involved a plot, with all the clues available to the reader. My friends were very patient to read and reread versions of the mystery to be certain the clues were not too few or too many, that the ending was logical but a surprise. And while I realized I could never hope to achieve the warmth and depth of non-human characters reached by my idol Mercedes Lackey in her Valdamar series, I wanted, needed, to bring the tiny papillon character in the mystery to life. I needed to keep Mischief alive and young as the character Sky in the book.

Immortalizing Mischief was one of the many objectives of the book. As the weeks rolled by, it was more and more apparent that my dearest love was aging fast. His little black half-mask had turned completely grey and the brilliant red over his ears and eyes had softened to a dusty strawberry blond. He still ruled his pack but it took more effort and longer naps in between his directive activities.

After rolling off the bed in his sleep one night, he became a clinging bedmate. I banked the far side of the bed with pillows to prevent another fall, but he insisted on sleeping with his six pounds on top of the cover and plastered against my body. Such a position makes it very difficult for me to move, and not at all conducive to my rest. Fallon, on the other hand, found the new arrangements imminently satisfactory since she now had most of the bed to herself. No matter how many times I put Mischief on the other side of the bed on his pillow, I'd always awaken in the night to find his softly snoring little body snuggled up tightly against my side.

He seemed to know I needed pushing on my editing efforts. His contribution to the book was to wearily drag himself upstairs at night and head off for the computer room instead of the bedroom. There, he'd curl beneath the chair at my desk and give me a look that said "Time for you to work and me to nap."

I was on the final edits to the book the night he went into cluster seizures and died. For weeks I battled my grief and Fallon's. She refused to eat or drink, spent most of the day and night curled in the bed she'd shared with me and Mischief. I begged and pleaded and hand fed her with tears streaking down my face. Finally after three weeks, she decided to take up where he had left off, and started eating and escorting me to the computer room to keep me company while I worked.

I made up my mind that the mystery, dedicated to him, would be printed and ready to send out as Christmas presents in memory of the little one who would not be around to write the Christmas letters this year. However, I guess I prayed too strongly for a challenge and a hill to climb, because the second half of the year seemed filled with obstacles that seemed to prevent my publishing plans.

I was obsessed with getting the mystery published. The trouble with obsessions is that they block out other rational thinking. So when I began to have troubles with my right knee, I ignored it until it was impossible to get up the stairs. By the time I finally sought help and learned that I needed surgery, I was hobbling around with a cane. Then and only then did I remember my plans years before to put a bed in the downstairs master bedroom, which I'd utilized exclusive as a sitting and TV room up till this time. So belatedly I decided to get an adjustable bed for this sick room, only to find that all stores have such 'functional' beds in the back of their stores -- way in the back. So far back that viewing them is almost an insurmountable feat when you're hobbling along with a cane. I grumbled my way through four stores, probably leading the sales staff to wonder if they were trying to assist a crazy woman, before finally settling on a twin size bed that did everything but talk. Fallon was not amused that there was no room for her on the narrow width of the bed or at the end with my bandaged and elevated knee. Nor did she appreciate the vibration function of the new toy. The heading element that was a part of the new contraption did little to help the pain in my knee, but the cats thought it had been bought especially for them and got more use out of it than I ever did. I especially disliked the nineteen-pound feline draped over my bandaged knee; it did nothing to improve my disposition. The offending 'large yellow dog' had finally remembered my vet's pronouncement that cats didn't know the meaning of 'no' and refused to respond to instructions to stay off the bed. He had to be locked out of the room in order to keep him from sprawling over my bad leg.

Somehow we got the book off to the printers, with Fallon's beautiful picture on the cover and Mischief's picture on the back cover. About the time the blue-lines came back for verification and one last shot at editing, an extra element of challenge had been introduced. Hurricane Floyd had brought days of drenching rains. Then high winds came through and dropped a 75-foot American Oak on the corner of the house. Happily, it only brushed the roof and slipped off into the side yard, making a wonderful, wooden, doggie climbing challenge for the gang. The root ball lifted up some seven feet into the air ripping the right back corner of the fence with it. Between phone calls to try and get tree removal services in spite of the heavy demand for such efforts in the area, I struggled with the loss of electrical power for several days. Editing blue-line isn't easy in the best of light. By candlelight it was a challenge that I'd just as soon not ever have again.

For several weeks, life because a series of games between me and the Astra gang to see how to keep them secure in the yard. They'd watch me limping along with my

Jean C. Keating

bandaged knee, cane sinking into the soft dirt every few steps, as I bumbled around the yard trying to patch the gap in the fence where the root had lifted up the wire. Then the minute I turned away, they'd rush to the area and prove their intellectual superiority by getting around my patch and wiggling under the fence once again. They never went anywhere, just ran up and down the fence on the outside of the wire, wagging tails and ears in doggie laughter and watching me scream myself hoarse.

And then suddenly the books arrived and I saw the product of my months of labor. I picked up a copy and admired Fallon's beautiful picture on the cover, and the dedication to my beloved Mischief, and cried at the picture of him on the back cover. Then I found a misused word on the first page to which I turned. A very serious and poignant poem was a clue and appeared in the book. Somehow what should have read *revealing* had slipped through the spell checker and appeared as *reveling*. I didn't know whether to laugh or cry. I settled for inventing a few choice curse words.

Annoyance cooled and I rationalized that I'd gotten exactly what I'd asked for: challenges. Did I forget to mention that there were limits to the level of difficulty I wished to encounter in this game of life? I guess I did. I decided I'd be more careful what I asked for the next time.

December, 1999

Dear Friends and Family,

As the elder statewoman of the Astra pack, I've taken over the duty of writing the Christmas letter. My beloved mate Mischief died on June 9, five  months after his 16th birthday. In the last twelve months of his life, he'd gone everywhere with Mama Jean: to Blacksburg for a Civil War weekend, where he stayed with Aunt Mary Ann and Uncle Larry [to the disgust of the Moore feline population], to the Metropolitan Area Papillon Show, where he fretted unless carried in a shoulder bag close to his human, and to meetings of the Chesapeake Bay Writers' Critique Group where he listened respectfully to everyone's work and kept any criticisms to himself.

An ice storm in January dropped four small trees on the left side of the house, and knocked down the fence. We lost power for almost 8 days. After months of dealing with repair people we'd about gotten things back to normal when Floyd came along in September and dropped a 75-foot oak tree on the right side of the house and took the rear and right side fences out. Mama Jean has taken to teasing the insurance company that they don't make gutters like they used to, after the gutters across the back of the house had to be replaced twice in a nine month period. There were some mild threats of 'moving to Arizona' after the second weather disaster, but Mama Jean doesn't like heat, so none of the Astra gang or I feel a need to worry about packing.

Mama Jean had knee surgery the end of July. It was slow healing and kept her hobbling around until well into September, but didn't prevent her finally publishing her first mystery. The book is named **Amorous Accident: A Dog's Eye View of Murder,** and was named for Mischief's brother, the first Champion bred by us. The book has been a great thrill, bringing newspaper articles, book-signings, and a wonderful sense of satisfaction to the top bitch of the house. It's dedicated to Mischief but it's my beautiful picture on the front cover that attracts people to look and buy. We all have high hopes of it bringing us enough money to fund our cookie budget for the new year.

Jean invented a few new curse words when she had to edit the blue-line by candlepower, thanks to Floyd and the tree dumped on the corner of the house. The cats and we canines provided plenty of heads to stroke to keep her blood pressure within limits, so we got through the chore finally and kept the book's release on schedule.

We're supposed to be publishing another book in a few weeks, but Jean is way behind schedule on that. Between trying to learn marketing [by doing everything wrong], and struggling with advertising [we could do it better but she won't ask for our help], she isn't writing the stories she'd sketched out nearly fast enough to complete them on time. I guess the Astra gang and I will just have to lend her a hand as soon as we get these cards out to you people, so we can move that project along faster.

Granny Kitty is doing wonderfully well. She's still getting around fine, enjoying a life of bingo, crafting, and sing-alongs. I agree with Mischief about staying as far away as possible during those singing sessions. Granny walks with a cane, but uses it mostly for swinging around rather than bearing her weight. For a brief period, a new psychiatrist decided to decrease her medication because she was always asleep by 8:00 pm when the doctor came to visit her. The decrease in medication resulted in a return of her paranoia, and she drove everyone around her crazy with complaints that someone, everyone [including the psychiatrist] was stealing her social security checks. Mama Jean and the facilities administrator both knew she got her checks and ignored her. The psychiatrist wasn't amused by her accusations, so he made a second and upward adjustment of her medications. She then resumed enjoying activities at the center.

Granny still wants the temperatures in the mid-80's, so Mama Jean just keeps her supplied with fleece-lined pants and matching tops. Last Friday when we were there, she was trying to wear three sets at once so she could show them off to her friends. I'm glad she had such a nice heavy 'fur suit', because otherwise none of us canines could bear the temperature in her room.

The rest of the gang and I are just another year older and better. Seven of the gang are now over twelve years of age, and Sunny and Misty are ten. We sleep more, run less, and still manage to keep Mama Jean and our nanny jumping to keep up.

From all of us, Merry Christmas and a healthy and happy new century.

Fallon

Champion Astra's Fallon of Bow Creek

Challenges

The first year of the new century brought everything I'd prayed for. Unfortunately, I asked for challenges to give life after retirement meaning, focus, purpose. Silly me! As the new century took off with gusto, I was reminded of another cliché: *I know God won't send more than I can handle, but I wish he didn't have so much faith in me!* I don't know why people denigrate clichés. Sayings get to be clichés because they are so often true.

January brought a blizzard, and two little puppies born during the fourteen continuous hours of snowfall. In Maine, eighteen inches of snow is nothing. In Williamsburg, this was a traffic-stopping event if nothing else. Fortunately power lines survived the storm, and there was plenty of light to see that the little male was beautifully marked with a wide white noseband and an evenly placed white blaze. The thin white blaze and uneven noseband on the little girl promised to turn into a near solid head at maturity. During a long struggle with tube feeding and sleepless nights, I named the little boy Winter Wonder and marveled at his resemblance to his great-grandfather Mischief who had died the year before.

When I lost Wonder after only forty days of life, I was devastated. He'd packed a lot of living into just a few short days of life. He'd demonstrated at only five weeks the papillon's favorite behavior of manipulating his human. I vowed to accept the lesson he'd offered and to make the most out of each day of living.

I owned a second home at this time, purchased for my mother when she moved to Virginia and now used as rental property since she was in a nursing home. Dealing with the rental-property caused frustrations that sapped my energies, so I determined the best plan of action to get it sold and out of my hair. Even while I fought to bring Wonder back from his final bout with respiratory difficulties, I called in a home inspector, had everything fixed that had been noted by the inspection, had the house freshly painted and put it on the market for a set price telling the realtor that no negotiations or concessions would be considered. It sold in one day. I regarded the sale as Wonder's gift to me for taking positive action, and turned again to writing to deal with my grief at losing him. His little story was published in a short-lived magazine entitled Pap-Pourrie but I wanted something more permanent for his memorial, so I renewed my efforts with the second book, one of short stories.

By the time my long-time friend, artist Bev Abbott, and I decided to attend the big national show of the Papillon Club of America in Nashville, Tennessee, we'd finalized plans to do a book together. Preplanning had worked well with selling the rental house, so I thought I'd do a bit of intelligent planning for the trip as well. I was worried that my aging station wagon Bluebelle wouldn't make the long drive to Tennessee, so I got a brand new rental for the drive. Stupid mistake! The rental broke down on the trip to Tennessee. The rental broke down on the way home from

Jean C. Keating

Tennessee. Bluebelle would have made the trip with half the trouble. I began to consider that the awful garden marker, passed down from my ancestor and now residing in my garden, might be more than I'd thought, might be some weird prayer altar that took a perverse joy in answering requests that were made in pity or anger. Something – maybe my long ago whining cries for challenges – seemed to bring opportunities I'd never anticipated or wanted.

Between delays for repairs and calls to the rental company for authorization, Bev and I discussed stories and ideas for illustrations for the planned creation. The plans were exciting but they made me miss my little fur children even more, so the trip was long and lonely in some ways.

I was delighted to get home again to return the complaining rental vehicle to its owners and to hug my little children-in-fur. Well, hug the dogs anyway. The two cats, Sunny and Misty, came near enough to turn their backs on me to make certain I knew of their displeasure at being abandoned for eight days. And admittedly the dogs were more interested in my luggage than in me. They busied themselves with sniffing through my dirty clothes and other packages for any sign of treats and presents.

Sunny seemed to decide that peeing in the bathtub was reasonable punishment for being left alone for a week. I filled the tub with Clorox to discourage that behavior and he promptly tracked the Clorox through the house, leaving a sinus clearing smell to the entire house and permanently lightened places on my carpet resembling paw prints.

I threw myself into work on the short story book. In addition to collecting stories from other dog-loving friends about their own favorite companions, I made certain that the biographies of each author were slanted to represent the unique relationship between author and animal subject of their stories. Before **Pawprints On My Heart** was published, I'd amassed stories of cats, a horse and one of a bird to go along with the many heartwarming tales of dogs that made their way into the book. Of course, my greatest pleasure was the picture on the cover of Fallon and the one on the back cover of Mischief.

After sleeping in a large pen downstairs during my week away, Fallon was happy to return to the luxury of our king size bed. However, she'd developed a habit of sampling goodies from her food and water dish during the night and tried to continue the practice upon my return. Unfortunately for the success of her plan, no water or food dishes were in the bed with us. She began falling off the bed in her fumbling around to find the dishes and I resorted to piling more and more pillows along the side and bottom of the bed to protect her. We were up to eight pillows by the time she finally returned to her normal habit of sleeping through the night. I was beginning to wonder if there'd be any room for me on the bed with all the pillows.

My papillon choral group can generally be relied upon to tell me when the squirrels in the next yard decide to move their nest or the wind removes more than two leaves from any tree, so the upheavals that continued to happen as spring progressed were greeted with a good deal of noisy energy. Just about the time I resorted to laser surgery to hasten the departure of a kidney stone of unusual tenacity, the washing machine decided to quit. Between a nurse in the house to help me and the repair man who made repeated trips to attempt to fix my antique washer, the Astra pack's voices got quite a workout providing the proper instructions and warnings to the two temporary staff on how jobs were to be done. The repairman suggested several times that a more appropriate expenditure of coins might be allocated toward the purchase of a new washer. This suggestion took on a whining plea just after one of the boys startled him with a high-pitched bark at his feet and he lost his wrench in the bowels of the washer. The nurse finally threw up her hands at attempts to keep my bed sanitary when I insisted that I couldn't possibly sleep without at least one if not three dogs to keep me company.

The nurse exited in defeat and left my home and bed to my Velcro buddies and me. The repairman managed to locate his wrench, put several patches on the old washer parts, and depart with a trail of noisy hecklers at his heels.

Summer came and rains vanished. Unfortunately fleas seemed to thrive in the now arid climate. In desperation, I had the shrubs cut back and the yard sprayed for pests. Holy was now approaching his fourteenth birthday, a quiet gentle lamb who tried his best to find a place of peace in the yard where he would not be bothered by the host of younger kin that always wanted to pull his ear fringe. Seeking a quiet retreat, he ducked under an azalea bush and scratched the cornea of his left eye on a recently pruned and sprayed limb. Repeated medication both in the eye and taken internally failed to halt the spreading infection and worsening tear. When the cornea finally ruptured, he had to have eye surgery to repair the problem and wear a tiny Elizabethan collar made of x-ray film to keep his busy paws away from the surgical site. He enjoyed the attention the newly acquired collar gave him, however, especially being able to smack the plastic collar against one of his granddaughters when one came too close to him for his liking.

Wonder's sister and littermate hit the show circuit and seemed, for a while, to be a shining success. She was named Winter Waltz and called Windi and her early shows were a testimonial to her call name. I managed to get **Pawprints On My Heart** published and began a series of book signings assisted by Holy's litter-sister Happy. I was just beginning to believe I must have imagined that my misguided cries for challenges the weekend of the Antique Road Show intrusion had been unwise, when Happy began to show signs of breathing difficulties. Further tests revealed an enlarged heart with a damaged valve. Thinking back I could only wonder if the three weeks she'd survived outside in snow and ice were contributing to her heart problems now. She took the heart medication in stride and was jumping up and down in my face to accompany me on the next book signing.

I'm no trainer. It would be more correct to say that I'm the trainee, since papillons excel in wrapping humans around their dainty little paws. So I take no credit for Happy's outstanding performance as a book-signing partner. But this little lady, somehow, seemed to understand that children and even adult humans might be frightened by rapid movement. I noticed that when anyone approached our table, she would simply freeze and do an Academy Award rendition of a stuffed dog. Except for those big ears! Her ears would flick back and forth, fanning the beautiful black fringes that had, of course, been specially groomed and brushed for the occasion. Only after adults and/or admiring children had reached to pet her would she slowly move her head to turn and lick their hands. I started to issue a command to 'Freeze' whenever people approached. It was more to teach her the word to go with her action in the hope she would pass her behavior on to the others in the pack than any need to modify her behavior.

As Thanksgiving approached, I decided not to take any chances that the dratted ornament in my garden might have a malicious power to turn my whining and ill-thought-thorough complaining into any more trouble. So one calm and sunny day, the pack and I spent most of the afternoon rearranging the now dreary garden. I reset the ancient garden marker into a different bed, surrounded by colorful mums. The move was accompanied by happy laughs and positive statements about the joys of fall. Of course two of the boys had to pee on the statue before I could get it settled. Windi grabbed off two of the blooms from the yellow mum, and ran from Ivory who was trying to grab them out of her mouth. Holy tried to eat one of the bronze blossoms, and Nikki tried to bury something unrecognizable in the dirt I'd just spread over the newly settled plantings. That's about normal for gardening with a pack of papillons. But I wasn't making any complaints about them, and I certainly wasn't whining about not having enough challenges in my life.

December, 2000

Dear Friends and Family,
    Christmas greetings from the Astra gang. Hope
your year has been as filled with excitement as
ours. Mama Jean says she could have done without a
 lot of the melodrama, but I
enjoyed myself thoroughly.
    I'm a great-grandmother.
Wish I could share my 150
photos with you, but Jean won't
copy them for me. So I'll stick to bragging instead.
Two of my grandchildren, Princess and Prince Val,
live with our good friend Aunt Phyllis. Well, they got
it together in the fall and produced four beautiful
babies, three little boys and a little girl.
    You'd have thought Mama Jean and Aunt Phyllis
had never been the humans of an expected litter
before. Aunt Phyllis sent out invitations to a puppy
shower, all our doggie relations attended, bringing
presents and their doggie relations. The humans

opened presents, played games, and generally had a silly old time of it. The canine members of the pack were much more sensible. They just ate up the finger food while the humans were busy with other things. I don't know why Mama Jean and Auntie Phyllis were acting so smug. I'm the grandmother of both the sire and dam, so I'm the great-grandmother squared, and I should get all the credit and most of the attention, don't you think?

The girl was tiny at birth and Aunt Phyllis had to supplement her food over the first three days. As usual, the humans I have to contend with overdid it. I think Aunt Phyllis and Mama Jean must have gotten growth hormones slipped into the milk supplement, because tiny Dottie is now the largest of the four grandkids and is never going to fit into the 'under 11 inch' limit for a show dog.

One of the tiny boys was born with a harelip and a cleft pallet. The humans would not listen to any professional advice on the unlikelihood of saving such a baby, and Auntie Shirley stepped in to actually do the hand raising and feeding of the little mite. Mama Jean and Auntie Phyllis named him Astra's Beguiling Bundle and called him Bunny because he charmed everyone who met him. But Aunt Shirley just calls him Bandit because he stole so much of her sleep. He's smaller than his siblings but has no trouble at all ruling Auntie Shirley's house and home. She's so attuned to his tonal whines, that she can easily distinguish his whine for needing to go out from his signal that he wants food or water from his cry for help when he misplaces his favorite toy, a graying [once white] cloth-covered bone he called Mr. Fuzzybone. I wish I did half as well with training Mama Jean.

The other two boys are just normal, which means they zip around too fast and make too much noise for my liking. I grumble a lot if they happen to bump me when our paths cross, but they mostly keep the younger member of the pack busy with their silly pranks.

I rarely get over to see Granny Kitty any more, because we're both in our 'nineties' – well, I'm sixteen plus in actual years but that's almost 90 in dog years – and neither of us likes to go out much. Jean and I made a special trip the other day, however, to visit. Granny was asked to be the star of a publicity video for the senior care facility. Of course, us girls had to get together to decide what Granny was going to wear. As the senior member of the Astra pack, I wasn't about to get left out of the excitement. So Mama Jean and I assembled in

Granny's room with donuts and coffee and all her outfits scattered about so she could pick the flashiest one to wear in the video. And it really, really wasn't my fault that I put the paw print of grape jelly on the pink outfit she finally wanted to wear. Don't let them tell you I was trying to get my signature into the video. I was just stretching to get to that last jelly donut in the box and that dratted outfit got in the way.

We've put up a lovely little tree and are getting ready for the holidays around here. Sunny the cat does not make decorating the tree easy. He has decided to become a gravity scientist. He's utilized any piece of decorations he could secure as his test items. No matter how many times he rolled one of the small toys off the side of the table, no matter how many times it responded to the pull of gravity and fell as it should, he would not accept the conclusion that gravity was working fine. He kept repeating his experiments until Mama Jean got annoyed and shook the broom at him. When he tried to extend his experiments to the entire tree, he really got the alpha female upset and she shut him up in his bedroom. The decorating went faster, but it was a bit noisy with all the racket Sunny made by flinging himself against the closed door to his prison.

Well, the tree is finally up and Mama Jean is adding some very pretty boxes beneath it that smell as though they may contain something of interest to me. So I think I'll close with a Happy New Year to you all, give her these letters to distract her, and go see if I can get into those packages before she catches me.

From the Astra pack and me: happy holidays and best wishes for a healthy and happy new year.

Fallon

Champion Astra's Fallon of Bow Creek

Billowing Sails

The winds of change blew the second year of the 21st century in with gusto. Life with an elderly dog began to dictate changes in routine around the Astra digs. Sixteen years had dimmed Fallon's vision. Until New Year's Eve I had neither realized nor would admit that the years had also taken her hearing. She showed no reaction to the holiday fireworks, though the remainder of the pack alerted, barked or just looked at me for reassurance with each celebratory explosion of Colonial Williamsburg's salute to the holiday.

The lifespan of papillons is longer than many breeds. Like most humans, I didn't want to think about the time when age would take its final toll on my cherished friend. I had noted, then ignored the graying muzzle and faded coloring on her head, the lack of spring in her hindquarters that prevented her jumping into her usual place when it came time to watch TV. I'd accepted as normal that she came to me, placing her front paws on my leg, and waited to be lifted to her favorite pillow behind me on the sofa. Suddenly forced to accept that she was now deaf as well as visually impaired, I had to make accommodations for her geriatric state.

170

Paw Prints Through The Years

On the first day of the new year I cordoned off a small section of the yard with x-pens so that Fallon could have a space for exercise that did not take her far away from my sight or her view of the door from the deck to the sun room. The younger members of the pack decided the structure represented a new game. So they got a running start from the other side of the yard, ran full force into the sides of the pen and jumped up to push it down. I repositioned it with large ground stakes and tried again. Fallon tottered around my feet as I worked on her new enclosure. The pack of juveniles retried the game of knock–the-pen-down but found the reinforcements too strong to allow any movement and lost interest. When placed inside the newly anchored enclosure, Fallon seemed content as long as I was nearby. On those occasions when I left her free in the yard with the rest of the gang, I observed more closely now that she took her cues from the remainder of the pack and came back to the door to be let in as soon as she saw or sensed the others returning. While the remainder of the group treated her with gentleness and compassion, I was more cautious of letting her out with the others. No matter how small and dainty the breed, dogs are still pack animals and a pack will turn on any member that behaves differently. I altered outings to make certain she was always in my sights when outside with the others.

With greater awareness of her growing feebleness, I watched her attempts to follow me around the house, and realized this was getting to be a chore she could not comfortably manage. It was not possible to carry her from room to room as I ambled about the house with routine tasks nor always practical to wait for her to follow me in her halting fashion. Left to her own decision, she still seemed to feel the obligation of all papillons to fulfill their role as companions and try to follow wherever I went. Despite her failing energies and advancing age, she ate with pleasure and enjoyed the evening's quiet time and TV sessions, though her snoring and my declining hearing necessitated turning the volume higher on the set.

One former friend went so far as to suggest that 'her quality of life was compromised, and I should have her put to sleep.' My response was rather calm, considering the anger I felt at the suggestion. I responded that most 'quality of life' arguments are put forth by humans who really mean they don't wish to exert the extra effort to care for an aging animal that has given the devotion and loyalty for all their years, and that I would never consider such a step until an animal companion signaled that they wanted to be released by refusing to eat or drink. I was indignant that a loving friend's existence should be treated so casually as to throw it away because age and infirmity imposed limitations.

I set about designing accommodations for my aging friend. I was hobbling around on my bad knee and silently expressing gratitude that no one wanted to bump me off for not moving with the body of a twenty year old.

For safety's sake, I secured a four-foot by eight-foot segment of the family room with another x-pen and put Fallon inside the enclosure with her bed, potty pads, and food and water dishes hanging from the enclosure. There she was safe and protected whenever I was writing or otherwise occupied. The remainder of the pack could communicate with her through the wire sides of the pen, but could not reach her to jolt her or hurt her. The arrangement served other purposes at the same time. Her food and water were now elevated which made it easier for her to drink and eat, and she could pick at her food and come back to it later if she chose. The fast moving members of the pack couldn't get to her food to take it from her. And since the wire pen barred her following me, she could relax and sleep in her bed without worrying that she needed to continue her usual Velcro dog thing. She was in the middle of everything but protected and secure from the usual chaos of the household. She could easily find her food and water without spilling it, and a potty area was readily available. She found it so relaxing that she was often sound asleep in her foam cushion bed when I scooped her up at night for a final outing before being carried to her pillow on the sofa back for TV or upstairs to our big bed for the night.

Imp, old Johnnie One Note, found the attraction of a full cup of food just past the barrier of a wire pen an appealing challenge. He would stand on three legs and try to paw the food from Fallon's cup through the wire enclosure and into his mouth. The small amount of food he got this way always seemed to be far more satisfying than the food from the same source that he was given in his own dish.

As winter merged into spring, another ultrasound of Happy's heart showed that the enlarged chamber diagnosed the previous year had gotten slightly worse, but her medications kept her comfortable and consistent with her name. She and I continued our efforts to find outlets for book signings. One of our finds was a delightful independent bookstore in Richmond that was ruled by a large, grey cat named Hamilton. I was thrilled to get my books in the store and to do a book signing there. Later checks of their web site showed that my mystery made the Top Ten list. We figured we'd never make the Top Ten on the New York Times Best Seller list, so we'd celebrate this one. The gang and I had a grand time commemorating this small achievement, toasting Hamilton [with Cokes for me and chicken stock for the gang] and the little dragon named Morgan who is the featured host and tour director for the web site for Creatures 'N Crooks. Happy garnered lots of praise for her continuing good sense and behavior with people who came to our book signings. She never failed to impress young and old with her rendition of a stuffed dog with movable ears. The only trouble was she began to think she needed to accompany me any time I went out the front door, which made Fallon and a few of the others in the pack a bit jealous.

In late spring, Happy and I were scheduled to do another book signing, but that Saturday morning I noticed that she was stopping to rest a lot on our trip outside. That lack of energy plus her failure to eat her dinner the night before or her breakfast that morning made me decide to leave her at home to rest while I took Ivory with me to help with signing books. Despite her disinterest in food, she was most annoyed that Ivory went in her place. And I was lost without her help. Ivory never learned nor saw any need to freeze, be still or stay on the table for that matter. People who bought books that day got a lot of paw prints where they weren't intended.

By Monday, Happy's failure to drink or eat had become cause for serious alarm. I rushed her in for blood work, and came home with her to wait for the results, since the sound of her heart seemed no worse than usual. By afternoon, I was beginning to panic because of growing signs of dehydration. By the time I rushed her back for sterile water under the skin, the results of the blood work told an unexpected but sad tale. Not her heart, but her liver had totally failed. She was gone in a few hours, with little warning and too little time to say goodbye.

The loss of his litter sister and soul mate sent Holy into depression. He refused to have anything to do with the rest of the pack and spent more and more time sitting dejectedly against the wire barrier of the x-pen near his mother Fallon. Thankfully he was small and light and I could often do household chores or write with him held in one arm, resting against my shoulder to comfort him.

Happy's unexpected death strengthened my interest in getting the members of the Astra pack together for a party. Fallon's 17th birthday seemed the perfect occasion for a celebration and reunion. I was overwhelmed and delighted with the response from all the extended family, those who'd adopted Astra puppies and others met through involvements with dog shows. I'd kept in touch with families with Astra puppies over the years, but few of them knew each other. So in addition to arranging for the food and the caterers, the decorations and the tents, I also had the fun of devising nametags to identify each human's relationship to the papillon they escorted to the party, and the relationship of the papillon guests to each other.

Of course, the Astra pack helped me ready the yard for the party. Every weed and unwanted sprig of plant that I dug up and tried to drag down to dispose of in the ravine was trailed and tugged on by at least three of the resident paps. Fallon had been joined by her elderly son Holy within the protected enclosure of their x-pen in the yard, which reduced the number of hinderers by two. Ivory decided not to wait on me to dig up offending growths, grabbed a low lying limb of the crepe myrtle and tried to tug the tree down on his own. Nikki decided it was more productive to tug her sister Little's tail. Fortunately, the crepe myrtle was mature enough to withstand Ivory's onslaught with nothing more substantial lost than a few blossoms. The yard looked very decorative with pink blossoms coloring the grass. Between laughing at my helpers and stopping every five minutes to recover a glove or a small hand tool that one or another had grabbed and tried to run off with, I figure it only took about four times as long to get the yard clean as it should have.

The day of the party, local friends began arriving early to help set up and get things going for the party. Friends got the two white tents set up, and tables covered in matching blue and white linens. Virginia weather in June can be hot and muggy, but it put on a special show in honor of my aging friend's birthday, remained sunny but cool and breezy, a perfect day to be alive and outside. With 31 dogs and 27 humans expected for the party, the guest of honor needed a central but protected area from which to enjoy her guests. So she had a bright new magenta rug spread beneath her x-pen, which was repositioned under the dogwoods to give her center stage for the party. Beneath the green canopy, the filtered sunlight showed off the colorful rug and the magenta and blue balloons attached to the sides of her pen. Her thick foam bed was covered in a new blue spread. Her son Holy joined her inside the x-pen, so that he too could enjoy the company without worry of strange dogs bumping him from his blind side.

For some, it had been six, seven or eight years since they had visited from homes far away. They stayed in touch through Christmas card and pictures, but had never been back until this party. Yet each papillon walked through the front door as though they recognized the place, came straight over to me with a friendly greeting, and then went looking for the big yellow cat. Sunny outdid himself greeting his long lost puppies, confident that their humans would be understanding and friendly also.

Soon most of the 31 dogs were wandering around the yard, entertaining the human guests and enjoying the opportunity to socialize with their own kind. The two rescues in the yard were just as much at home as the rest of the crowd. Only a tiny Maltese named Jazzie, who'd accompanied her two humans to the party, refused to socialize with the paps or leave the safety of one or the other of her humans' laps.

My friend Kathy Godfrey had come from Raleigh, North Carolina for the party bringing a little dog she'd gotten through Papillon Club of America rescue. Her little girl, renamed Bijou, was a little dismayed at all the activity and people but quickly developed a keen interest in the doggie buffet set out on a rug at the end of the table holding the humans' food. One of the resident paps took up a position behind the large bowl of ice water set out on the dogs' buffet, as the self-proclaimed hostess for the event.

Enticing smells from numerous dishes cooked especially for the dogs attracted the pack. Kathy had also brought a giant blue plastic butterfly serving dish with five large compartments as a present to the birthday girl. That was filled with five different types of specially cooked dog treats, the most popular of which was an anchovy seasoned dog biscuit cooked for the occasion by another friend who wisely left her Cavalier King Charles pack at home. One of my favorite photos of the day showed the dogs calmly lined up waiting their turn to choose a treat from their table. Nothing was more fascinating or heartwarming about the day than the party manners displayed by the paps who attended.

The birthday girl and her son had many attentive servants to make certain their food bowls within the protected area of their x-pen were kept filled with doggie treats. From time to time, many of the canine guests wandered over to touch noses through the wire of the pen and extend their greetings to Fallon and Holy.

The Astra gang's vet and friend was mobbed by the many dogs attending the party, causing him to tease that they seemed a lot friendlier in the yard this day than they had ever been in his office.

Despite the fact that few of the humans had known each other before the party, conversation seemed to come easy to these doting attendants of butterfly dogs, and the afternoon seemed to be enjoyed as much by my guests as by me.

The euphoria of this gathering carried me through a difficult decision in mid-year. I had grieved over the loss of a little puppy named Winter Wonder, but accepted the reality now that his sister might never finish her championship because of her solid colored head. Repeating the breeding raised my fears that I might get and lose another little one. But the match-up of pedigrees between Nikki and Anne Carmichael's multinational champion Scooter was just too perfect to deny. So I set about to arranged for another pairing of these two.

It always seems that breedings which are not wanted happen without effort. But if you really, really want to get a litter between two dogs chosen by human standards for health, adherence to breed standard, outstanding temperament, placement of white marking, ear set and about a hundred other considerations, a modification of Murphy's laws takes over. As in *anything that can go wrong will*! When it was time to send Nikki up to visit with Scooter, Anne had just accepted four extra dogs as guests at her place while their owners went to Europe. She was reluctant to bring Nikki into her home with all the others there. She suggested that she send Scooter to me instead, and I happily agreed. The minute Scooter came into the house, Nikki went out of season and said 'Forget it, I've got a headache," to Mr. Scooter. Nikki's sister Little decided she liked Mr. Scooter's looks, so I called Anne and we rearranged our thinking. After all, Little and Nikki were littermates, so the pedigree match-up was the same, if not the color and attribute matching. Just about the time I was absolutely certain we had a good mating between Little and Scooter, Nikki changed her mind, little sister Peaches ran off in the azaleas with the visiting swain and suddenly I had three ladies-in-waiting counting on their toes up to the magical nine-weeks.

Murphy's corollary: *the thing that goes wrong will be that which causes the most trouble!* Oh, goodie! Nine weeks later, I had three mother dogs and seven puppies to deal with. Only eight days separated the birth of the three litters. Since the three mothers were full-sisters and the father was the same beautiful, multi-national champion I was suddenly faced with seven, beautiful fat worms that somehow look very similar. Six males and one female! Of course! I ordered little girls.

I foolishly reassured myself that people with other breeds deal with six male puppies in a single litter and have no problems. So now along with maintaining three playpens for three very proud mother dogs, I had to do detailed drawings of each little fat worm to tell them apart. The joker who dreamed up the plan of different colored ribbon around puppies' necks to identify individual puppies never met a determined papillon dam. Little, Nikki and Peachie would remove little ribbons faster than I could attach them.

At four weeks, two of the males looked so similar that when I return them to their playpens and mothers after a joint play outing on the rug, I failed to check the drawings and returned them to the wrong mothers. Neither Nikki nor Little were very amused and quickly set me straight on which belonged where. My eyesight might have trouble telling Zack from Driver, but their noses had no such difficulty. Thankfully, by seven weeks the marked difference between a tri-colored and a red was readily apparent even to my inferior visual and non-existent olfactory senses.

Puppies had always charmed my mother, and I often took one or two with me to the nursing home to let her play with them. Mother seemed unable to focus on pictures of these last ones and uninterested in holding them when given an opportunity now. To me, her physical health seemed to continue stable through the fall, but I sensed that her mental state was dimming. I was wrong on both counts. She remained mentally alert until almost the end of her life. She recognized me and would talk to me up until two days before her death, suddenly and unexpectedly from renal failure, the day after Thanksgiving. She'd wanted her ashes taken back to Georgia and buried beside my father. Three wonderful friends made the long trip with me.

Jean C. Keating

It was comforting to return home to seven active, happy young papillons that made the cat tired with their playing, dissuaded me of any plans for a decorated tree this year, but kept each new day bright and happy with their combined antics.

December, 2001

Dear Friends and Family,

Somehow it got to be the end of the year! Don't know exactly what happened to the time, but my dam Fallon tells me I have to write the annual letter from the Astra gang this year because she's

 too feeble. And being a gentle and obedient son, I always do what my dam and my Mama Jean ask of me, so I'll try to catch you all up on the past

year's happenings.

Sadly, we'll spend this Christmas without Mama Jean's mother, Granny Kitty. After a frisky and seemingly enjoyable year of bingo and sing-alongs, she'd been excited to appear in a promotional video for the skilled care facility where she'd lived for the last four years. Then in late October, her kidneys completely shut down, and she died in her sleep on November 24, 2001. So Mama Jean began the holiday season with a sad trip to Georgia to return Granny Kitty to the quiet family cemetery in Lexington, Georgia to rest by the side of Grandfather Zack who died in 1981.

My dam turned 17 on June 8th of this year, and on June 9th, Mama Jean threw her a big outdoor party. Fallon and I had a wonderfully colorful enclosure on a magenta mat with blue, pink and magenta balloons tied to the x-pen, which protected our sleeping rolls, water and food from the 31 canine and 27 human guests that attended. It was set in the dappled shade of the dogwoods, but in the center of the party. It was wonderful getting to see so many of my kin at once, and I certainly enjoyed all the canine goodies that were available.

The second of my grandsons by Val and Princess went to rule his own home in early February, but was back to introduce his humans to all of us for the party. His humans, Karen and Charles, call him Bandit, though Mama Jean named him Astra's Bonnie Bairn of Redd.

As Christmas day approaches, my dearest dam is old, mostly blind, mostly deaf, but still hanging on and bossing Mama Jean around with demands for food and attention.

None of the grandchildren managed to obtain any championship titles this year, but the last of my three grandsons by Val and Princess did manage to get his junior pilot's wings. When Dash went to live with Charlie and Flo Sippel in Rhode Island, Jean and his new parents made certain his trip home would be in comfort. So he flew first class, charmed all the flight attendants, and was presented his wings by the captain upon arrival at his new home. Now Dash was a bright little boy, but I wouldn't want to ride with him. Just between you and me, he couldn't run around this house without bumping into something on the way from point A to point B.

My sister, Happy Habit, also left us suddenly this past spring. She'd been diagnosed with congestive heart failure in the fall of 2000, but was dealing with that nicely, excited about her job as supervisor and partner at Mama Jean's book signings. I miss her most of all. My littermate and best friend, she was always my partner in play or rest. In more than fourteen years, we'd never had a cross bark between us!

My daughter Dixie, owned by Mama Jean's friend Barbara Foley, gave the two proud human grandparents four beautiful puppies last year, including a little girl named Trinket who took a Group IV from the Puppy class in her first AKC show this spring and finished the requirements for her

AKC conformation championship at 10 months of age. So, of course, Mama Jean decided to increase the population around here some more by asking the same sire, Scooter Carmichael – who has more national championship titles than we have toys – to help us out by siring some more puppies with several of my other daughters. The only trouble with Mama Jean's planning is she always forgets to consider the water in Williamsburg. It always gives us boys! Not girls! So this fall, I've had six bratty grandsons running around here giving me all kinds of trouble. I keep packing their bags and inviting the garbage men to take them, but Mama Jean keeps catching me before I can get rid of the rapid moving, noisy little creatures. They pull my tail and my ears and make so much noise I think I'm living around a beehive! Hard to believe, Fallon and Mama Jean expect me to write any kind of a letter with all that going on, but I'm trying.

Mama Jean joined Weight Watchers this year and has managed to lose some weight. The Astra gang and I think that's great, because now she feels like spending more time walking with us. Of course, it does limit the caliber of leftovers we get around here. Are they still making steaks? Or is chicken the only meat left in the world?

Well, I think you've had enough of a flavor of life here in the Astra digs for the year. Maybe we should try to write more often. Things seem to get a bit long when you only do this once a year!!!

From all of us, best wishes for a wonderful holiday season and a peaceful and healthy new year.

Holy

Astra's Hardly Holy

Passages

January was the longest month in the year. ***Pawprints On My Heart*** was a finalist for the Maxwell Award for Best Fiction of 2001 awarded by the Dog Writers' Association of America [DWAA]. Waiting until the awards were announced in early February took all of my patience and then some. Naturally, friend and associate editor Dot Bryant, artist Bev Abbott, her husband Ira and friends Cindy and Larry Torgersen were in New York City with me for the awards. The book didn't win, but we all had fun anyway.

The DWAA's awards banquet and ceremony coincides with the Westminster Kennel Club Show each year, so we stayed to see the toy breeds shown at the Garden the next day. Getting into the show was a lesson in patience – of which I had none. The security precautions in place for that large of a gathering after the 9/11 disaster resulted in a two-hour delay at the doors, but did nothing to diminish the crowds that came. Inside, Madison Square Garden was a human gridlock. Somehow the six of us managed to work our way to a position at ringside when the papillons were shown, and Ira got some wonderful pictures of the champions who came to show their hearts out. I got some great shots of the back of Ira's head. None of our crew wanted to fight the crowds for much longer than the breed events, so we bailed out before groups that first night and came back to Virginia.

Nanny Barb had her hands full between puppies and the older members of the Astra pack while I was away in New York, so she was glad to see us home a day earlier than planned.

By now the struggle to find names had been overcome. The 'D' litter had been named Divine Diva [called DeeDee] and Designated Driver, and I had resisted all pressures to let them go to other homes.

Fortunately for my sanity, Little's crew of four boys coincided with the 'E' litter. Can you imagine the difficult with finding names contain duplicate letters if the alphabet had been an 'X' or a 'Z'! Earthbound Eagle went to Richmond where Mike and Janet just named him Tazz Shipley. Extra Edition went to Raleigh, to become Andy and Karen's little boy Cody. Eager Embrace was supposed to stay home, but Ralph and Prissy convinced me that he would be better off spending his life as Rudy Lampert. I did manage to hang on to Endless Energy, called him Zack, and spent a considerable amount of time in the months and years to come, trying to prevent him ripping the fringe off DeeDee's ears.

The daughter of a dear friend had her eye on Peachie's singleton puppy, and finally succeeded in getting my agreement to let her take little Feffer [Astra's Feather Force] to train and show at the upcoming Metropolitan Area Papillon Club [MAP] event a few weeks following Westminster. I reluctantly agreed, cautioning her that with his solid head, little Feffer would never make a show dog. She insisted she wanted him to practice at showing, that she wanted no other. In the months and year to come, she would remind me of my assessment of him as 'just a pet'

Jean C. Keating

each time he won this show or another, especially when he won his first major of the two major show wins needed to be named an AKC champion.

Winter Wonder's full brother, named Astra's Designated Driver and called *the Driver* proved to be a very promising show dog. He debuted at MAP in the company of Peg Quarto who had taken him a few months earlier to train for the show ring.

I attended with my aging Fallon. By now Fallon needed to eat about five times a day just to sustain herself since her digestive track was beginning to fail in its job to extract nourishment from food. Still, she loved to eat and to awaken me at all times of the night to request food if none was readily at hand in her dish. She was cordial and friendly to all who came around at MAP, glad to accept a friendly pat on the head but hearing none of the noise and relying on smell alone now to help her identify her friends. But the failing eye sight and hearing, the graying muzzle, and the feeble responses to caressing hands told her friends there that she'd come to say her last goodbyes to them.

Her death in March, two months short of her 18th birthday, was more than Holy could stand. He was her oldest son and had been her constant companion since he'd lost his sister Happy. He refused to eat and resisted all veterinary help until he followed her to the Rainbow Bridge ten days later.

My tears weren't even dried before another little butterfly arrived in need of love and help. Jock's first ten years of life had been filled with ups and downs. A kind and elderly owner had given him love but exposed him to a badly behaved grandson who had kicked the little five-pound dog in the head, breaking his jaw on both sides. The work to repair his jaw had left him deaf, without any teeth, and very fearful of children. Adjustments for this little deaf butterfly were difficult but humorous. His fear of being hurt motivated him to seek a secure hiding place before curling up to rest, but in true papillon fashion he wanted to follow me from room to room. So he couldn't settle into any place unless he was certain his body blocked a younger member of the pack from getting out. That way, the younger member stepped on Jock on his way out to follow me. It took a few months for everyone to adjust so that he felt certain he could rest, but still know when I left the room. I also learned what to move in any room to get him from his hiding place when bedtime or mealtimes came.

Meanwhile Peg and the Driver were making history for the Astra pack.

To be eligible to compete in shows sanctioned by the American Kennel Club [AKC], a dog must be at least 6 months old on the day of the event. At beginning shows, young puppies often get their experience and season their skills by competing in the six-to-nine month puppy classes where the lack of an adult coat doesn't hamper their competition against seasoned mature dogs. But winning a puppy class doesn't bring any points toward a championship.

Show points are based on the number of dogs competing for the win at a given show. Wins at large shows may bring an award of three, four or even five points [the maximum awarded at any one show] toward a championship. To qualify as a conformation champion with the AKC, a dog must win at two shows of sufficient size to justify at least three points, a major show, which dog show people refer to simply as A MAJOR. Show dogs pursue events in which they can acquire their major wins.

Puppy winners must eventually go up against seasoned, mature dogs with adult coats to compete for the points. Which my darling little charmer did! And he won! He won four major shows from the 6-9 month puppy class, one of them a 5-point Major, to earn the right to put Champion

Jean C. Keating

before his long name. And he did it by the tender age of eight and a half months! I floated about two inches off the floor for a good month after his championship attainment.

Shortly after his nine-month birthday, he entered the ring as a Champion, won the breed ribbon, and went on to take a second place in Toy Group. I wiped happy tears from my eyes when Peg called to share the news with me, and thanked my lucky stars that I'd decided to repeat the breeding that had cost me the loss of little Winter Wonder.

I was still trying to effect communications with Jock and enjoying the euphoria of Driver's show success, when another old dog joined the pack. A phone call one night from the Rescue Chairperson for the Papillon Club of America asked for help for a ten year old papillon left in need by the failed health of his elderly owner. Initially I intended to serve as transport and temporary foster home for Charlie, whose owner had fallen and broken a hip. At 81, she survived but required a skilled care facility, so Charlie was left homeless. Kindly neighbors transported him to my door from his home four hours away, but the dog that arrived was not what I'd expected.

Though the AKC papers provided by a pet store proclaimed him to be a papillon, he was much larger and heavier than any pap I'd ever seen; he weighed 25 pounds and had tiny ears like a sheltie. We began potty training, but ten years of being allowed to go in the house was a serious mind set to overcome. We walked; he'd take care of business, but save some to leave on my den floor. A blood screen showed kidney values so bad that he was not expected to live more than a few days. He didn't read that book. An ultrasound revealed a huge gallstone. He started medication to keep the bile thinned and continued in his lumbering way to fit himself into life with the Astra pack. He would let anyone take even his favorite treat, his Greenie, or anything else away without complaint. Of course, he'd

190

immediately come over to my knee and request another.

If begging another didn't work, he had a foolproof ploy that did. He quickly found that he could sit beside the door to the closet in my computer room, pretend to scratch a non-existent flea, thump tail or leg or both against the door and send his light weight pack members for the front door, alert-barking all the way. While they were rushing to the outer limits for defense of the house, he'd walk behind them calmly retrieving his greenie or whatever toy he wanted.

And people who come to visit wonder why I never answer the door when they knock! Well, cell phones were invented to call me from the curb if you expect me to open the front door.

December, 2002

Dear Friends and Family,

Gosh! Has the year gone already? Doesn't seem possible that it was twelve months since Holy sent holiday greetings to you all on behalf of the Astra gang. Mom says that when you're over the hill, the slope is downward and goes faster and faster. Don't know who she's calling old around here. I just turned fourteen on December 9th, so she can't mean me.

But that does mean I'm the eldest of the Astra pack now, so it is my job to write the Christmas letter. I enjoy the bed dog privilege as senior dog — I get my pick of the down pillows — much more than the writing chores of the office. But I'll do my best.

As you will have gathered from my being responsible for writing this year, Holy and our dam, Fallon, are gone. Fallon tried very hard to make it to her eighteenth birthday. She wanted to see if Mama

192

Jean could plan an even bigger birthday bash for her since her 17th was so special. But living with a body that was about 104 years in human terms just got to be more than it was worth. Older brother Holy was happy that many of his grandsons had gone to their own forever homes leaving him more quiet time, but he missed his dam who was his sleeping companion and elderly buddy too much to stay, so ten days after Fallon left, Holy joined her at Rainbow Bridge.

But it isn't lonely or empty around here. Two new/old faces came to join the Astra pack. Charlie and Jock were rescues whose elderly owners could no longer keep them, so they're now running with the rest of the gang in the house and yard

One of our books, *Pawprints On My Heart*, was chosen as one of three finalists for best dog fiction of 2001 by Dog Writers' Association of America. Mama Jean was really happy and went off to New York City to the awards banquet, along with friends Ira and Beverly Abbott, Dot Bryant, and Larry and Cindy Torgersen. Although the book didn't win the big prize, the gang got a fun trip to the Big Apple and went to see the Westminster Kennel Club show the day after the DWAA banquet. I was a bit miffed because I wasn't included in the party. Ira,

Beverly and Dot got some wonderful pictures of the papillons at Westminster. Mom, on the other hand, spent a good deal of film capturing the backs of other peoples' heads. I think she should give up picture taking, since she isn't much good at it.

Unfortunately, Mama Jean has been dragging her feet and hasn't finished the book about our lives, which is to be called *Paw Prints Through The Years*. We're getting tired of waiting, as you might guess. Not only are we not getting a lot of walks because she spends so much time calling the computer bad names, but she spent her time writing stories about other things, like the cats. Now Sunny is an all right guy, but his picture is on the net in a story Mama Jean wrote, and not my handsome mug. Now you know that can't be fair. And to add insult to that, the cat story is nominated for another award by Dog Writers Association of America [I think Mama Jean didn't tell them it was about a cat] and she's going off to NYC again for the 2003 awards banquet. No walks because she'll be gone and the story and the pictures are about the cat! I think I'll go eat the cats' food, just to show them who's in charge here.

On top of the cat story, Mama Jean also took on the responsibility for a regular monthly column for the national magazine for papillons. It's called Rescue Corner and is about other dogs but not us. Well, our new brother Charlie was the subject of the first column, but I'm still waiting to get my picture in these things. Mama Jean reminds me that I'm not a rescue, but keeps promising that some stories in the new book will feature me. But do you think she'll finish the book! Oh, no. Just keeps on writing on other things.

Gardening for the year has been a joke. What the drought didn't get, some of the puppies did. In mid-fall, we tried pots of pansies on the deck since they would last into the cold part of late fall, but the puppies just decided these were a collection of small sand boxes and promptly dug them all up. Don't know what the younger generation is coming to. I certainly was never allowed to do such naughty things when I was a pup. But the gang and I turned the yard into a crater-filled moonscape just to give Mama Jean something to do in filling the holes. That'll teach her to ignore me as a subject of her stories.

I guess about the biggest news around here just now relates to the two young puppies born in 2001. Zack and Driver began their show careers together and faced off a lot at dog shows, taking points away from each other. Mama Jean finally pulled Zack and brought him home, and left the field to Driver. Well, the little rascal finished his championship from the puppy class at eight and a half months of age, has already taken a placement in Toy group, and is going to compete in the Westminster Kennel Club show in February with Auntie Peg Quarto at the other end of his lead.

Our friend Bev Abbott took some beautiful pictures of the Driver and has used one to paint the cover for the upcoming book about the Astra gang. Now if Mama Jean will just finish writing the thing, I can practice my pawagraphing routine and help out with book signings.

Hope your year was happy and prosperous. On behalf of the Astra pack and our Mama Jean, I wish you the happiest of holidays and a bright and safe 2003.

Ivory
Astra's Ivory Illusion

The Warmth of Family

Another Saturday morning and another dog show, this one at Richmond's Showplace. In twenty-two years, the chairs haven't gotten any softer and there's more of me to try to fit into the hard seat. Otherwise, this day is a lot different from that one more than two decades ago when I fell in love with a little papillon named Vinnie. I know most of the people at ringside and in the ring, and I know most of the dogs and the sires and dams that produced them. The judge is very special, one of the rare breed that is qualified to judge all AKC recognized breeds, not just a few; one of the handful of judges qualified to judge Best In Show. The experience and confidence shows today; he's relaxed and smiling, radiating warmth and making the event the fun and joy it should be. The dogs respond to his friendly demeanor with wagging tails and the exhibitors visibly relax under his competent and happy directions.

My pride and joy, the Driver, is entered in Breed competition today. He and his partner, Peg Quarto, are up against their usual three competitors. They beat each other regularly, so this is just another adventure and competition. His first cousin/half-sister Trinket is in the ring with her owner Barb Foley; his buddy Jinx and Maureen Dyer, with whom we shared a room in New York during the Westminster show, are here today also. And he's up against the fourth ranking papillon in the country, Nike and his partner Pat Harris. Nike looks particularly focused today in spite of the noisy confusion of the metal roofed Showplace. My presence at shows has seemed to be bad luck for my little champion. While none of his big wins have ever happened when I was at ringside watching, I'm not about to stay away today. This show is special for more than breed competition. It is home turf, being only fifty miles away, and a lot of friends are here both in the ring and sitting at ringside.

Driver's daughter Bella, owned and handled by good friend Shirley Hardee, is competing from the nine-to-twelve month puppy class, and needs only two more points for her championship. Feffer and Driver's other daughter, Driving Miss Daisy, are also in the ring with their owner, Shirley's daughter Karen King. Daisy is competing from the six-to-nine-month puppy class. Another of my dogs, Driver's first cousin Zack, is competing from the open class with Time Traveler's owner, Margaret Van Cleave, on the other end of his lead.

Two more of my dogs are at ringside, held in the adoring arms of their humans, John and Vivian Harrell. The two are pets but are here to share the fun and cheer the show members of the family on.

The day's events bring many happy moments. Bella wins the points in bitches for her third major and her championship. Little Daisy wins her six-to-nine-month puppy class and another blue ribbon. Now that Bella has finished her championship, she won't be competing against little sister Daisy for the points. Now younger sister Daisy will have a better chance at capturing the points for her championship. When the final ribbons are passed out, Driver has taken the Breed, his daughter has taken Winners Bitch and Best of Winners and completed her championship, and half-sister/first cousin Trinket has taken Best of Opposite Sex. And if this isn't enough of a high, several people come over to congratulate me on my numerous quotes in an article on papillons in the current month's issue of Dog World. Many noted the introductory paragraph, mentioning that I've authored three books on the breed and asking about the third book. Shame faced, I have to admit I haven't yet finished it. But nothing can diminish my pride in my little dog family and in the recognition, however small, of my writing efforts.

My friend Phyllis and I split up and separately prowl the vendors looking for papillon things we can't live without. Somehow we manage to arrive back at the group ring with the same large hedgehog as the toy of choice to take home to our four-legged children. The identical choice is a source of much teasing between us. While I'm fairly certain that the combined talents and numbers of my brood are sufficient to deal with the mass of the rather largish toy, I tease Phyllis that her two butterflies, Princess and Val, may not be up to the task of taming this large of a plaything.

The toy group showing is a joy to watch even if Driver doesn't even make the judge's short group of contenders for the placements. With the show's conclusion, Phyllis and I brave the oppressive heat and humidity of late afternoon to reach our hot car and drive home tired and happy.

Back at the Astra digs, Charlie the rescue pounces upon the largish hedgehog and decides it must be for him since he's the largest thing in the pack. His attempts to drag it back to his large crate to hide it from the rest of the gang are complicated by the two or more, smaller papillon bodies attempting to carry off one or more of the legs in other directions.

Jean C. Keating

The electronic mail from the day brings rewarding news about two other members of the extended family. Carolyn has now taken a foster dog, one of the 225 rescued from a puppy mill in North Carolina, to share her home. Resident queen of Carolyn's house, Priss [Astra's Regal Refrain], is a bit put off by the intrusion of Dreamweaver but will soon revert to normal papillon behavior of attachment and affection for one of her own breed. Kathy, Carolyn's friend and mine, lost Tutu [Astra's Picture Perfect] at a very early age, adopted Spring from PCA rescue and renamed her Bijou. Now Kathy and Bijou have opened their homes and heart to another papillon in need, little Lucky, who was also rescued from the puppy mill in North Carolina. Remembrances of the many friends who share a love of these delightful butterfly dogs bring tears to my eyes, but a warm glow to my heart.

Today has been exciting and rewarding, but leaves plenty of room for more challenges tomorrow. Driver will have other chances to pursue a group placement, and maybe someday a win in Group. I still have my book to finish. Most of all, there are fond memories of a happy day shared with many friends.

Retirement has become what it should be, the best of life which utilized the experiences gained from living and the memories of past achievements to enrich the present. And it includes a dream for the future.

Beverly S. Abbott, Artist

The colored plates in this book are available as prints for purchase. Contact Bev Abbott, Artist at babbott@visi.net

The giclee prints are created with archival, pigmented inks and may be printed in a variety of sizes depending on the size of the original oil paintings from 4" x 5" to approximately 11" x 14 ". Prices will vary but are usually in the range of $10 to $40. The art may be printed on paper or canvas.

Commissions are accepted for oil portraits of your favorite pet. As of the publication date of this book, the prices for oil portraits begin at $125 for an 8" x 10" painting on hardboard, unframed. The artist welcomes inquiries for further information.

Nature, Pets and People in Oils, Graphite, Pen & Ink

E-Mail: babbott@visi.net
HOME PAGE: http://members.visi.net/-babbott

Chapter 1:
The medical research lab was filled with personnel and equipment
engaged in recording and evaluating the' homicide scene. The buzz of
human voices was augmented by the soft cries of several guinea pigs
in a cage against the left wall and whines from two dogs in slightly
larger cages on the floor in front of the portly figure directing the
operations.

Kevin Andrews, his protruding stomach straining the buttons
on his shirt, was glad that the body had been covered. Even to the
seasoned lieutenant of detectives, the corpse had been a stomach
turning sight. At fifty-seven, Lt. Andrews thought he had seen
everything, but the sight of a tall, elegantly and expensively suited
male, secured in some sort of metal rack used for animal experiments
was new to him.

Unfortunately, disruptions to his plans by a homicide
investigation were anything but new. In deference to his Captain's
urgent call a short time earlier, Andrews had quickly altered his plans
for a Friday off. His anticipated leisurely morning, as well as his
planned three-day visit with his godson, had been hastily canceled.

Trying to simultaneously redress and explain the necessity for the change of plans on the phone to his godson, Jonathan, was responsible for two additional aggravations. A shoe lace on his dress shoes, earlier broken and quickly replaced with a new one, proved to be a slightly different color of brown to his keen eyes in the bright lights of the medical lab. His relatively new navy suit, in a larger size than previous suits, was all too comfortable, but the white dress shirt he'd hastily chosen from his dresser was uncomfortably snug and no amount of re-tying of his tie would hid the strain placed on the buttons to hold the shirt front closed.

His momentary indulgence in petty gripes was quickly arrested. A darkly handsome figure stepped over several scattered boxes on the floor and approached Andrews, notebook in hand. Andrews relaxed slightly at the sight of the striking face with its high forehead and full head of near-black hair. If he had to be saddled with a tricky case like this one, he could have asked for no stronger backup than this young sergeant.

Slender, with dark eyes and complexion, Bart Foster was affectionately known as 'Black Bart'. Full eyebrows arched perfectly over large, intelligent eyes framed by long, curled lashes. Women found the eyes disarming, sometimes a convenient tool in ticklish homicide investigations. Bart's manner, like the heather gray worsted wool suit which fit his athletic frame to perfection, was professional and crisp. He wasted no time with preliminaries now.

"Death seems to have taken place between ten last night and two this morning," Foster said placidly. "Doc should be able to tighten the time a bit as soon as he finishes the liver temp test. The body wasn't discovered until this morning at eight-thirty. The victim's secretary has a key to the lab, usually opens things up when she arrives." He might have been describing a bus schedule for all the emotion he allow his voice to show.

"Identity?"

"Michael Porter, Chief of Research here at the Institute, according to preliminary identification by the secretary, Ms. Piper Morgan."

"The one who discovered the body?" asked Andrews.

"Yes Ms. Morgan had the presence of mind to call the Hospital Administrator, Dr. Harold Ketterholt. He says he took one look into this room, and ordered the door locked again until the police could respond," said Sergeant Foster.

"So any prints on the door would have been obliterated by either Ketterholt or Morgan." Andrews' hand reached up to scratch his left ear, a routine with which Foster was very familiar. It indicated Andrews' annoyance at the destruction of possible evidence.

"Well, I guess we can be thankful that someone showed the presence of mind to seal the room and wait for our arrival."

"Ms. Morgan was badly shaken by the discovery of the body. I've instructed her not to talk to anyone until you've had a chance to question her. She's in a office across the hall drinking a cup of tea at the moment," continued Foster. "Dr. Ketterholt has returned to his office, but will be available whenever you need him. He said he would notify the victim's wife personally. I took the liberty of requesting he contact the head of security for the institute and have him standing by. I also asked that he furnish us with a list of names and addresses of staff occupying offices in this building."

"Efficient, as usual, Foster," acknowledged his superior. "See if any of that crowd in the hall outside may have heard or seen anything unusual. I want to talk with Twill for a bit, then I'd like for you to sit in with me while I question Ms. Morgan and Dr. Ketterholt."

With something that sounded like a 'yes, sir', Foster turned to the door of the lab to carry out Andrews' request. The pudgy lieutenant of detectives allowed his light hazel eyes to wander lazily over the littered scene of the murder once more. He slouched rather than stood, and his lethargic look fooled many who met him for the first time. His fellow law enforcement officers in the room knew from long experience that the lazy eyes missed very little.

A bent figure replaced the sheet over the head of the corpse and straighten to reveal a tall stick of a man in a rumpled suit that seem to float around the thin body. The walking skeleton's head was as bare of hair as his body was void of flesh. A slight fringe of gray hair partially encircled the head on sides and back, leaving the shining bald top sparkling in the overhead ceiling lights of the lab. Behind thick lens in horn-rimmed glasses, small green eyes turned to focus on the detective lieutenant. At a slight nod from Andrews, Dr. Paul Twill, police surgeon for the City of Richmond, picked his way between police personnel and litter to reach the lieutenant's side.

"Well, this one is a mess," Twill began. "Glad they put you in charge. Someone didn't like this fellow -- didn't like him a lot!"

"What can you tell me about the cause of death, possible description of murder weapon, and time."

"Well, we'll have to wait for an autopsy for the official findings, but if you want my best guess ..."

"Give me what you've got, and in plain English too. Not all this mumbo-jumbo you spout in court," said Andrews testily.

"Based on the liver temperature test, he died somewhere between 10:15 pm and 10:35 pm last night. He was rendered unconscious by a blow to the head. Something dull. It left a large bump but didn't break the skin. After the blow, and probably while he was still unconscious, he was trussed up like you saw, arms and legs bound behind him with tape. He was secured in that cubic metal frame over there, his head rigidly held by medal rods and a leather harness. A tube was inserted down his throat and secured by a generous amount of tape. Then some type of acid was poured down his throat."

"Acid? Damn! Any idea what kind?"

"Again, you'll have to wait for the autopsy for that. But something very corrosive," said Twill. "Like I said before, someone didn't like this guy! He regained consciousness early on, possibly lived four or five minutes after the acid was poured down his throat."

"Damn," Andrews repeated, "never hear of this one before. Are you telling me the acid killed him?"

"Well, in one way or another. Shock from the pain, acid spilling onto the internal organs through a hole or holes in the esophagus ..." Twill analyzed.

"Spare me the details," Andrews said emphatically. "Would it have been possible for a woman to have trust up the victim and secured him in that contraption over there?"

"Well," Twill drawled, taking time to weigh the question before responding. "Yes, if he were unconscious at the time. It would have been difficult for a woman, but possible, I guess. But it's a very brutal way to kill someone. Fairly turns my stomach, and you know there's not much that gets to an old police surgeon. I've seen everything after more than twenty years with the force in this town, but this one gives me chills. I guess I just can't imagine a woman doing this," he admitted finally.

205

"Kipling would disagree," Andrews answered somewhat enigmatically. "More deadly than the male."

Twill's face registered his momentary puzzlement before the meaning of the reference registered and a one-sided smile lightened his thin face.

"Ah, yes! *The female of the species!*"

"Still, there has to be a reason for such a brutal method of killing," Twill continued. "Do you think illegal drugs might be involved?"

"We'll dust the area, but it seems unlikely. I doubt if drugs would be kept in this guy's personal lab anyway. This being a cancer research and treatment center, certainly there are plenty of drugs around. But I don't see why anyone would be looking for such here. And the method of killing rules out an attempt to extract information from the victim."

"You're comfortable with your estimate of the time of death?"

"Yep! You're fortunate there. The temperature control in this room makes it easier to estimate. I'd say death occurred somewhere between 10:15 pm and 10:30 pm, maybe as late as 10:35 pm, but that would be stretching it."

Andrews mumbled something that passed for thanks.

"OK. I'll take the body now and get the autopsy process started unless you need me further here."

"Go ahead," said Andrews, already turning his attention to the progress of the team dusting for prints and clues.

"Any idea how much longer you'll be, Dunfort?" Andrews remarks were addressed to a tall, fair-skinned youngster who was busy dusting a nearby lab bench for physical evidence. Long red hair was pulled back in a pony-tail and light freckles dusted a short, tilted nose. Despite the trim look of a three-piece camel suit, the young officer looked even younger than her twenty-four years.

Andrews remarks startled the young women but she recovered promptly and replied, "Probably another hour at least. I've never seen so many prints, hairs, and other stuff at a scene before. I guess it's the animals, but it certainly looks like a lot of people have been in and out of here since the last time this place was given a good cleaning."

"All right. Make it as quick as you can. Then seal this place off until further notice," Andrews instructed.

"What about the lab animals, sir?" Dunfort's eyes looked worried.

The cries of the guinea pigs continued. The two dogs had ceased to whine, but both sat expectantly in front of the doors of their cages, soft liquid eyes following the movements of the officers and Andrews.

"Aha, yes! The probable eye-witnesses!" Andrews walked over to stand in front of the guinea pigs' cage. The black-and-white one was making all the noise, he decided. Now he saw why. The fur was gone from the back of the little animal. Strips of raw, inflamed skin were oozing moisture and causing the tiny creature great pain. Little wonder that he continually cried. The other five guinea pigs seemed uninjured but very fearful.

He crossed to the larger cages on the floor holding the two dogs. The larger one resembled a black shepherd Andrews had owned as a child. It stared at him with soft, expectant eyes but did not retreat when he approached. The smaller one resembled a shaggy mop, wolf-gray hair matted and dirty, one ear flopped almost over its right eye. The smaller dog plainly expressed anxiety at Andrews' approach and retreated as far as the back of his cage would allow, but made no outcry.

"Now if you could only talk," Andrews muttered aloud, "what you might be able to tell me." He would not admit that the sight of these animals in cages and obviously destined for experimentation touched him deeply. A tough lieutenant of detectives had to maintain an image, especially in front of members of his team.

"We'll see, Dunfort," said Andrews. "Obviously, the animals have to be cared for, but we can't return them to the institute just yet. Not until we're through with the room. Keep the room secured until I tell you different."

"I'll be in the administrator's office or questioning witnesses," he announced. Anything to get away from the pleading eyes of the two dogs.

The little guinea pig was still crying softly as Andrews left the room.

The following story from **Pawprints On My Heart** is reprinted here for your review and enjoyment.

Who's In Charge Here

by Jean C. Keating

The Papillons of today are descendants of the dwarf continental spaniels of the French royal courts. Tiny, light-boned and ever ready to get into pranks, they are a never-ending source of enjoyment and wonder. They also have tremendous strength of will and they never forget that they descend from royalty. The word imperious often comes to mind and conversation when discussing these elegant little 'fur-people'.

My first Papillon took over my life two months before her first birthday. Her full name was Debonair Maaca Choice. Within five weeks, she added the title Champion to the front of her name by prancing herself to wins at numerous dog shows. Her method was to march in the ring, look the judge right in the eye and say very plainly in body language, "I'm here. I'm the best. I want the ribbon, so send the rest of these also-rans home!" By two years of age, she'd taken over my bed, produced two sons to carry on her legacy, and managed to keep us all in line without the slightest matting of her silky, black-and-white coat. She was a lady and a queen. You could almost hear her talking in the royal first person plural.

Her second born son was named Mischief Maaca. From the moment his eyes and ears opened, he proceeded to live up to his name. He was all the things his royal dam was not - loud, brash and vocally assertive. He appeared to boss everyone around and the remainder of the pack usually gave him his way. The Queen was always nearby – with a look that conveyed, "We are not amused at anyone or anything that upsets the Prince!"

209

Mischief was almost two years old when friends came to visit bringing along their nine-month old Scottish terrier, Malcolm. As my human visitors and I stood around the living room discussing afternoon events and evening dinner arrangements, the Papillon pack and one immature Scottie milled around on the floor at our feet. Malcolm spotted a chew stick on the floor that looked appealing and moved toward it. Mischief immediately rushed to defend the chewie with loud growling and posturing. Scotties seem to process information at a much slower rate than the lightning-quick Paps, but Malcolm was steady in his advancement against the posturing Mischief. Human conversation refocused on the contest of wills exhibited between Pap and Scottie.

Malcolm's steady advance was met with increasingly loud grumbles and growls from Mischief, but in the face of an adversary that outweighed him 16 pounds to 5 pounds, Mischief retreated to continue his fussing from the safe position behind my legs. Satisfied at last that he understood the lay-of-the-land, Malcolm claimed his chew stick and settled down on the rug to enjoy his prize facing the vocalizing Papillon.

I was not concerned with 'family honor' but did want to insure that my young Pap's continual growling did not escalate into physical contact in which one of the two young dogs might be hurt … the one injured most likely to be my smaller fur-child. I made certain both were on leashes and returned to discussing dinner plans with my human guests.

The Queen had other ideas. Out of the corner of my eye, I noted her quiet but confident approach to within three feet of the Scottie. Making certain she had his attention, she settled gracefully on the rug and began to chew on another rawhide stick she'd brought with her. To my guests, this meant nothing. The toy box in the corner of the great room was loaded with doggie stuff of all kinds. But I noted the oddity. This was the first time I had ever known the Queen to bother with toys or chew sticks. She expected them to be offered with her dinner tray but never went looking for them otherwise.

The Scottie chewed more slowly on his recently acquired trophy as he focused more and more on the one being enjoyed by the Queen. Entrapment might not be a word the Queen understood, but she obviously understood the concept and how to apply it effectively.

Finally Malcolm abandoned his prize all together, and arose to check out the one being enjoyed by the quiet, black-and white dog in front of him. He approached confidently to within a head length of her muzzle before his advance was finally arrested by a low, soft growl from the Queen.

The Scottie's thought processes could be read as if a movie was running in slow motion. He stopped and looked pointedly at the Queen. She returned to quietly chewing her toy. He took a step toward her, only to be stopped by a second, low warning growl. He looked back at Mischief who still fussed loudly – from a safe distance behind my legs. Malcolm looked at the chew toy he'd contested with Mischief and won. He looked again at the calm lady dog in front of him. "Ah. No problem," he appeared to reason. "All that posturing and the other one backed off. No problem with this quieter one." So Malcolm grabbed for the chewie in the Queen's mouth.

Quick as a rattlesnake's strike, the Queen dropped her chewie, nailed him with a full mouth of teeth across his long, reaching muzzle, and administered another growl that only an experienced mother dog can deliver. Then before he could shake his head she'd retrieved her prize, returned to her prone position and resumed chewing her rawhide stick.

I couldn't help it. I laughed aloud at the poor Scottie youngster. He shook his head in disbelief. He looked at Mischief, still growling at him, but doing nothing. He looked at the Queen, calmly chewing on her prize and making not a sound. He shook his smarting muzzle and finally sought the comfort of his owner's side, still puzzled by the conflicting signals he'd read. But I'd guess that next time he'll spend a bit more time figuring out just where the power really lies in dog packs.

His brief visit with the Queen and her heir-apparent hopefully taught him the difference between real control and the noisy behavior of a "wannabe." I hope he grew, in time, to appreciate her teaching. After all, anything I needed to know about group dynamics I learned from my Papillons.